AMERICAN BADASS ACCOLADES

Chacon brings us a new style of zombie in this hilariously entertaining ZomCom. Forget the shambling undead of Shaun of the
Dead or the manic frenzy zombies of World War Z, "American
Badass" delivers Ron, a zombie with ethics and personal hygiene
concerns as well as the usual obsession for all things brain. I love
how this manages to combine zombies and humor without going
into B movie camp realm. The delivery is spot on, and zombie Ron
is unlike any other character I've come across. It made for a very
enjoyable, entertaining read.

How can you not enjoy a work by an author who can paraphrase
Jane Austen and the Princess Bride in a zombie story that takes
place in Las Vegas? This book is not only funny, but you will appreciate the subtle intellect hidden within the prose.

I laughed, cringed, snorted and wanted to grab a sanitizing cloth.
This is so off the charts from what you expect in a zombie read.
It's funny, with all kinds of politically incorrect moments, idiotic
people, ridiculous situations, bloody bone dipping and of course
brains. It was just what I wanted, dark humor.

American Badass is a crazy, hilarious, well written zombie comedy.
It's also unlike any zombie novel I've ever read, and I've read a lot
of them.

The real life struggles of an average zombie make us review our
own values and why we are on this earth. Is it all worthwhile? Is
something else possible after life? Brain soup for the soul.

50 SHADES OF BRAIN

AMERICAN BADASS 2

50 SHADES OF BRAIN

AMERICAN BADASS 2

JEFF CHACON

WOODEN STAKE PRESS

Published in the United States by Wooden Stake Press, LLC
Denver, CO
www.woodenstakepress.com

ISBN 978-1-940936-16-1

On and on and on and on, what side are you on?
- "Left of the Dial"
THE REPLACEMENTS

PRELUDE

ood evening, dear reader, and welcome to "American Badass 2: Fifty Shades of Brain." This novel has nothing to do with that other 'Fifty Shades' book, fortunately or unfortunately, but is instead a sequel to "American Badass," a Vegas zombie comedy published in 2014 (and soon to be a feature film!). So if you've come to this page looking for bondage, dominance, and BDSM in a book that is going to sell 125 million copies worldwide, you're in the wrong place and should ask for a refund on your purchase. But if you've come to this page looking for laughs, chortles, and guffaws in a book that is going to sell 12.5 copies citywide, you're definitely in the right place and this author wants to have your babies.

When we last left our beloved characters, Ron Watson was a zombie and a reluctant Internet meme with a useless duct-taped-to-his-body right arm, Maria was a pregnant zombie trying to snack on any human she could find, Jim, clad in a green fluorescent 'Girls Direct To You' t-shirt, was not dead, and Stella still thought her dad, who she loved very much, was a fucking asshole. And they were all packed into a 1968 El Camino SS with chrome rims, speeding through the Mojave desert away from Las Vegas towards a better future…

Until they turned the car around. Because nobody, living or undead, ever really leaves Las Vegas. It's the Roach Motel of American cities; people and zombies check in, but they don't check out.

But that's not where "Fifty Shades of Brain" starts. No, dear reader, this book starts several fortnights later. KILLZ (Kill, Impale, Lacerate, and Lay waste to Zombies), the government agency in charge of eliminating zombies, has disbanded, because Ron's popularity has made it acceptable to accept zombies, and zombies are accepted in everyday society. Well, tolerated, really. Like a big brother tolerates his little sister when his friends are around. That is to say, they live uneasily amongst humans. Like native Americans in our own country. Uneasily, but peacefully, for the most part.

And then some stuff happens.

So build a fire, grab a blanket, ask your favorite flair bartender for a cocktail, and settle in, dear reader, as we bring you..."50 Shades of Brain."

CHAPTER
1

Vegas Valley View Memorial Park and Mortuary (VVVMPaM) is a dreary oasis in the Mojave Desert. Dreary because it contains 98% dead people – 2% staff – and oasis because it has more green grass and lush landscaping than should be allowed in any natively brown and dusty place like the Mojave Desert. Of course, Las Vegas itself is no "normal" brown and dusty place; no, in this haven of dowhateverthefuckyouwant for adults, green grass and lush landscaping are virtually the norm. Especially when the norm contains 98% dead people.

Willie Green knew this; he was the landscaper for Vegas Valley View Memorial Park and Mortuary, and the directive from his bosses was and had always been, "make the alive people think their dead people are going to be very comfortable here, using plants and shit!" And Willie understood this directive, especially the 'and shit' part. Sure, being a landscaper meant you planted plants, but selling the idea that this was a nice place for you to put your grandfather three feet underground forever took a special kind of 'and shit' salesmanship genius that not every landscaper had.

Willie had it. Vegas Valley View was as green and lush as any oasis in a desert ever was, with native and non-native plants...ah, hell, who are we kidding? Everything at Palm Valley was non-native. Nobody likes their relatives buried with cactus. And everybody who was anybody in the Las Vegas Valley paid exorbitant amounts of money to leave their dead relatives at VVV, amongst the succulent Florida palms, the lush Asian irises, and the ebullient California eucalyptus trees. In fact, when asked why they wanted to put their grandfather three feet underground at Vegas Valley View instead of Vegas View Valley Park and Mortuary (VVVPaM), just down the street and one-third the price, most people simply replied, "it's the plants and shit."

December 1st started out just like every other day for Willie Green, caretaker; it sounded better than 'landscaper' to Willie, and when your employer is an international consortium of financial companies based in another country, you figure you can call yourself whatever the fuck you want, because who's checking, right? On this day, he rose at his usual 6am time, shit, showered and shaved, made his daughter's lunch for school, checked his son's math homework, dropped them both off at the bus stop at 7:45 am, and drove his 1967 Pontiac Firebird down Nellis Boulevard to make it to work at 8:40 am, just like every other Tuesday. Except, of course, this was not every other Tuesday. This was Tuesday, December 1st, and things were about to getting really weird up in this bitch.

CHAPTER
2

Jeremy Hybert met Kathy Ahern for the very first time at this year's Harrah's Labor Day Pool Party; she was a party pit dancer at the blackjack tables and he was a lifeguard at the pool. They were both young and attractive, living in Las Vegas and working fun Harrah's jobs while they figured out what they wanted to do with their lives, and now they were on their first date. Jeremy picked Kathy up promptly at 7pm – lifeguards have to be prompt – and took her to dinner at a sushi place – SuSuSushiO – in north Las Vegas, where they spent the evening getting to know each other enough to know that they wanted to get to know each other more, so they went for a nightcap at The Zombie Lounge, a small bar near their apartments in north Las Vegas.

The Zombie Lounge, set in the corner of a strip mall in the northeast corner of Las Vegas, had a faux English pub feel to it; dim lighting, dark wood paneling adorning some of the walls, British green paint adorning the other walls, oak floors that were new in 1958, and cocktail waitresses who looked like they were also new in 1958. It was not the hippest place in Las Vegas, but when you live in Las Vegas you tend to stay away from the Las Vegas Strip and the touristy hip places, because when you spend all day entertaining/serving/protecting tourists, the last thing you want to do at night is spend more time hanging out with them. Thus, The Zombie Lounge. A local's place.

"You ever been here before?" Kathy asked.

"No, but I've always wanted to try it."

"Yeah, me too. It looks cool from the outside. And everybody likes zombies." Kathy flashed Jeremy a 'play this right and you're going to get fucked tonight' smile; at least, that's how Jeremy saw it. But he was a guy, so every look from a pretty brunette said the same thing to him. You're going to get fucked tonight, Jeremy.

The cocktail waitress came over to their small round table, hacked up a lung and said, "Welcome to The Zombie Lounge, home of the blood orange cocktail. What can I get for ya?"

"Vodka soda for me," Kathy said as she grabbed Jeremy's hand under the table.

"I'll do a...vodka soda as well," Jeremy said as he smiled at Kathy. Vodka soda wasn't his usual drink, bourbon was, but Kathy's hand fit nicely into his, and when somebody's holding your hand you sometimes order the same drink they do. Don't judge.

The cocktail waitress, who was wearing what looked like a blood-stained outfit to go with the theme of the place, wheeled around back to the bar to get drinks. Maybe she didn't 'wheel'; maybe it was more of a 'waddle,' given her age and girth.

After another hour of small talk – Kathy's family was from Hawaii, but being the oldest of five kids she took off after high school and ended up in Las Vegas, while Jeremy's family was from Texas, but being from Texas means you wanted to live anywhere else, please, so he took off after high school and ended up in Las Vegas as well – and a couple more vodka sodas, Jeremy looked around, realized the Zombie Lounge was almost empty, save for the two couples on either side of them, and went in for the money shot: The Kiss. Kathy's lips were delicious, he thought, like fresh peaches, and her breath in his mouth was invigorating. Kathy, on the other hand, thought Jeremy tasted like Chex Mix, but she liked

Chex Mix, so this was not a bad thing. Jeremy put his hand on her breast as he savored her flavor; her breast was subtly supple and amply ample and fit into his hand perfectly. Kathy, on the other hand, put her hand in Jeremy's crotch and realized what he had wasn't going to fit into her hand at all. No, Jeremy was a Ball Park Frank; plump when you cook 'em. And he must have been cooked, 'cuz he was certainly plump.

"Click." Kathy must be undoing his pants, Jeremy thought, to let his manhood out from behind its curtain. Good thing, too, 'cuz even though we are in a bar, Jeremy thought, Little Elvis needs some air. Yes, he called his penis "Little Elvis." Don't judge. Very much.

"Shwoooot." Jeremy must be undoing his own pants, Kathy thought, to let that Ball Park Frank off of the barbecue. Good thing, too, 'cuz even though we are in a bar, she thought, she wanted to feel it. She was going to have to use two hands!

Out of the corner of his eye as he prepared to let his meat and two veg out to play, Jeremy saw the couple at the table to his east get up and slowly approach Jeremy and Kathy's table. Out of the corner of her eye as she prepared to grab something big and strong, like Little Elvis, with both hands, Kathy saw the couple at the table to her west get up and slowly approach Jeremy and Kathy's table.

What the fuck?

Jeremy and Kathy looked around and realized there were no windows in the Zombie Lounge. They also realized, at the exact same time – they did have a connection, after a successful night of first dating; a connection that, in a different scenario, might have led to a lifetime of love – that those clicking sounds had nothing to do with sex; no, those clicking sounds were the sounds of the front and back doors of the Zombie Lounge being locked.

They also realized, a few moments too late, that the bloodstained outfit adorning the decrepit cocktail waitress was stained with real blood.

CHAPTER
3

ortly Elvis woke up from his nap and immediately craved a peanut butter and banana sandwich, like he always did. "Portly," after all, was his nickname, not "Skinny Elvis," "Captain Elvis," Midget Elvis," or "Mexican Elvis," like some of those other fucks at the Thursday Night Elvis Night or even the Friday Night Elvis Night at the Bourbon Room. Thus, he was hungry…and he felt like shit. Like maybe, just maybe, seven was not the magic number of Mai-tais last night, maybe he should have held it to three or four, but when women are buying your local Elvis impersonator drinks is your local Elvis impersonator going to turn said drinks down? Hell no! He's an Elvis impersonator, he more than likely doesn't have much money! Free drinks must be consumed!

So PE, as his friends called him, felt like Graceland had transported itself from Memphis to Las Vegas and had landed on his head sometime in the night. Repeatedly. And his hunger had awakened him; he could always depend on his hunger to awaken him. He hoped The Colonel – his roommate, who was a Colonel Tom Parker impersonator, if you can believe that – had stocked up on Jif Smooth ("Choosy Moms Choose Portly Elvis," he always said), peanut butter, and Chiquita bananas. PE always had a thing for Chiquitas; the name reminded him of the bonita Latinas the real Elvis would meet on his South American tours, back in the day. Chiquitas always treated Elvis very, very well. Allegedly. PE had never been to South America, so he couldn't know for sure, but he had read up on Elvis history. Elvistory, as it was known in the Elvis impersonator circles. And Elvistory indicated that Elvis had a thing for bonita Latinas. Thus, PE did too. Gotta keep it authentic, right?

He looked up; the ceiling in his napping room was red silk, like it always was…except it was exceptionally close to Elvis' face. He swiveled his eyes to the left and to the right, hoping to see The Colonel holding court in the living room of his two bedroom apartment on the outskirts of Las Vegas, just shy of the Ring of Foreclosure. PE called his living room The Red Silk Room, after a room at Graceland, and he put red silk up on the ceiling – like at Graceland – and this is where he had obviously laid down for a quick nap. It was his Friday afternoon tradition; he'd lay down in the Red Silk Room on his second-hand red velvet couch and he'd drift off to sleep dreaming of South American women and Jif Smooth peanut butter. And wake up hungry. Like today.

But this was somehow different than his usual nap. PE rolled over to look at his television, which was tuned to stream old Elvis movies on Netflix half the time (Elvis movies helped him sleep)… and got stuck. Somehow. What. The. Fuck? He was fat, of course – no, he was Portly, as he'd tell his female fans, who didn't seem to mind. No, they especially didn't mind his ample girth when they came back to the Red Silk Room after a show to get a hunka hunka burnin' love with a portly hound dog – but stuck? The Silk Room has nine foot ceilings! And PE wasn't that fucking tall! He laid back down, tried to rub his eyes to clear his head, and got his hands stuck between his corpulent belly and the opulent ceiling of the Silk Room. Something wasn't right.

And who the fuck farted? The smell…PE inhaled semi-deeply and threw up in his mouth a little bit. That wasn't a fart; that was something dead. The Colonel had a cat who had died a couple of months ago under the couch on a Monday, and by Wednesday it smelled like this. It was a smell that wasn't easily forgotten.

Portly Elvis held his breath so he didn't have to smell the dead thing, lifted his head slowly, and struck it on silk. That's when he realized he wasn't going to get his peanut butter and banana sandwich anytime soon...because he was in a box. Not a cardboard box; no, PE knew that feeling because, prior to discovering he could make money performing as Portly Elvis five times a week at Bourbon Room in the Venetian Casino and Resort, he was homeless. Well, 'homeless' in the loosest definition of the word. He actually had had a home the whole time he was 'homeless'...a box. A cardboard box, underneath the P1 level of the Harrah's parking garage. This, today, right here? This was no cardboard box. This, he realized, was much more substantial than cardboard. Hell, this might be waferboard, even. Damn.

He unstuck his hands from his belly and lifted them up and felt the ceiling of the box, which lifted slightly. PE paused, not knowing what was on the other side of the box ceiling, and tried to imagine possible scenarios that would have had led to him being in this box:

Terrorist attack? Not likely. If terrorists were going to attack the USA again, surely they weren't interested in a formerly-homeless fat Elvis impersonator, right? If they were, PE thought, he didn't understand terrorism or the motives behind it at all.

Box assembly plant mistake? Like maybe he passed out on the box assembly line and ended up in an assembled box? Again, not likely. He didn't work at a box assembly plant, nor did he know anybody who did.

Angry ex-girlfriend? He hadn't had a girlfriend in a few years, angry or otherwise, and he was almost positive that every girl he had ever dated had gone on to find the love of her life within a week of dumping him (he was pretty sure he was directly or indirectly responsible for four marriages and nine children), so there really was no sense in them coming back to find him, a man (only in the most technical sense of the word) who had never found the love of life and had, in fact, at one time, literally lived in a box. He was pretty sure every one of his ex-girlfriends was too preoccupied with their gorgeous husbands, huge mansions, and handsome children to focus on the man who made all that possible by being a shitty enough boyfriend to dump in time to find much greener pastures.

Unable to imagine a scenario that would lead him being in this box, Portly Elvis pushed on the ceiling of the box a little more and saw light, but heard no sound. He pushed a little more and saw brown dirt and sky; okay, this wasn't the Red Silk Room. The Red Silk Room had walls and a ceiling, not brown dirt and sky. He pushed again and opened the top of the box as far as it would go; yep, sky. And dirt. Dirt walls, even, about two feet tall, all around him, leading up to the blue Las Vegas sky. At least he assumed it was the Las Vegas sky; it did have that tint of lost hopes and shattered dreams to it, so it had to be the Las Vegas sky. The stank around him wafted up into that sky....except he could still smell it. A bit more faint, but it was definitely there. Something must have died in this box.

He lifted himself up, or rather he tried to lift himself up. He was fat and he wasn't the strongest Elvis in the world – he obviously hadn't been to the gym in awhile, given his girth – so it took everything he had in his puny little Portly Elvis arms to sit himself up in this box...in this coffin.

COFFIN? He turned his head left and right; yep, this box was a coffin, all right. PE had seen enough scary movies – it was his other Netflix obsession – to know that this was a coffin. And that he, Portly Elvis, was dressed to die. Black wool suit, black silk tie, white dress shirt, nice shoes. Not his normal polyester jumpsuit, definitely. He scrunched his face until he looked like a pug; surely somebody was fucking with him. He pushed himself up a little higher so his head was above the dirt walls and looked around.

Cemetery. He, Portly Elvis, entertainer of millions…okay, hundreds of thousands…okay, tens of tens, he, Portly Elvis, was in a fucking coffin in a fucking cemetery in the fucking middle of the fucking day. And he stunk.

This was not just any cemetery, either – this was Vegas Valley View Memorial Park and Mortuary (VVVMPaM). PE recognized it from the time a few months back where he was actually paid to be the funeral officiant for a lifelong Elvis fan who had seen several of PE's shows and had passed on to the great Graceland in the sky (PE actually used those words in his eulogy). The main thing PE learned from that event was that it's fucking hot as the outreaches of hell in the mid-summer Vegas sun whilst you're wearing a black polyester jumpsuit. He should have gone with the white one that day.

His arms rested from all the thinking, he lifted himself out of the coffin, stood up, and stepped out onto the VVV grass. Skinny Elvis and Midget Elvis must have been behind all this, because those fuckers were jealous of PE. Let's face it, when you think of Elvis you don't think "skinny" or "midget." You might think "normal sized," like Elvis in 1956, but Skinny Elvis was so skinny he barely filled out a child-sized jumpsuit. And Skinny would eat and eat and eat and eat and that fucker never gained a pound; meanwhile, if PE so much as looked at a doughnut his ass grew three sizes. And Midget Elvis had to shop for his jumpsuits in the kid's aisle at the Elvis Impersonator store, which made him crankier than normal, if you can imagine a crankier-than-normal midget. So Midget and Skinny and Portly had a rivalry of sorts and pranked each other whenever the opportunity arose.

And this was obviously one of those opportunities. PE must have found some fancy-ass clothes somewhere and gone out with the Elvi (Skinny, Captain, Mexican, and Midget) last night, like they tended to do after their Thursday night shows at Bourbon Room. They wandered around Vegas like an Elvis Gang, posing for pictures with Elvis fans and drinking their favorite drinks at their favorite bars, which were plenty. Based on his current condition, PE must have had more than plenty peanut butter and banana martinis, 'cuz he knew Skinny and Midget couldn't have pulled this prank when PE was sober. He must have passed out and slept through the whole thing.

Those motherfuckers were gonna pay.

CHAPTER
4

STATUSCARD:

Ron – Zombie.
Maria – Pregnant zombie.
Stella – Teenager.
Jim – Zombie, and lovin' it!
Watson Fetus – Gestating.

A pelvic exam, an ultrasound, and BRAINS! Ron Watson's half-naked zombie girlfriend Maria was lying face up on a brand new granite island countertop in a brand new four bedroom, five bathroom house in the Ring of Foreclosure on the edge of Las Vegas, her panties on the brand new oak wood floor, her pregnant belly protruding into the air like the only hill in a flat Midwestern suburb, a doctor hunched over her, listening to her belly as if it contained the meaning of life. To Ron, it did. To the doctor...well, Ron wasn't sure he was actually a doctor. None of the Las Vegas hospitals Ron called took Zombie Insurance, the only insurance Ron had, so he asked his daughter Stella if she knew somebody who accepted that insurance and could perform all the necessary pregnant woman checkups. Stella, being as industrious as she always was, made a few phone calls, and here we were. With some guy with slicked back hair and a pronounced jowl, hunched over Ron Watson's half-naked girlfriend, in a house a bank owned, but didn't really want to own. It was certainly complicated, but somehow necessary, Ron thought. With all that had happened to them recently and her zombie condition, he didn't want to take any chances on Maria's condition...outside of trusting her diagnosis to some guy who looked like he spent his days off tooling around with the Vegas mafia. Don Doctor, Ron started calling him in his head.

"She's pregnant," Don Doctor said, after listening to her belly and examining her jumbly bits, as only a doctor or a really close boyf...no, really, only a doctor would do this. Ron liked female jumbly bits very much, but there's a fine line between pornographic and gynecological, and Don Doctor was definitely not on Ron's favorite side of that line.

"No fucking shit, doc, we can all see that." Ron's best friend Jim said. He had been absentmindedly turning the brand new garbage disposal on and off, like a child in an elevator, pushing the buttons for every floor. And he looked like a child not in an elevator, but in a school production of 'West Side Story;' slicked back hair, black leather jacket, wallet on chain. Ron wondered if he had been taking dressing tips from Stella. Or an Elvis impersonator. 1954 Elvis, before he started wearing jumpsuits and muumuus and shit.

"Is she going to be okay?" Ron asked.

Don Doctor, who wore a Motley Crue 'Doctor Feelgood' t-shirt and a pair of jeans over black biker boots and, outside of his jowl, had a very fit physique – are there *any* fat doctors? – turned to face Ron. "She's going to be fine. Based on her size and the baby's heartbeat, she appears to about 30 weeks along, and the baby appears to be doing fine. You want I should give her an ultrasound?"

Baby? Ron's head exploded. This was a baby? A human baby? But...

"Did you say baby?"

"Of course. What the hell else would it be?" He looked at Ron like he was Arnold from 'Different Strokes' asking Willis what he was talkin' 'bout.

Ron looked over at Stella, standing in what was going to some-day be the eating nook for a first-time home buyer looking for a first-time home to raise a family. She was smoking a cigarette and slowly shaking her head.

"Well, Don, of course. Baby." Ron knew he had to play along.

"My name's Vito."

"Of course it is."

Vito's faced scrunched up like he had just had an entire can of bitter beer in one gulp and he turned to Stella. "Your dad, is he -"

"No, Vito, he's just a little emotional, from the pregnancy and stuff, you know." Stella was once again very good at covering for her idiot father, Ron thought, because while they had Zombie In-surance and were using it, Ron and Maria had agreed beforehand to not disclose to Don Doctor that they were zombies. Because while Don Doctor accepted Zombie Insurance, he wouldn't *treat* any zombies. That policy was written on his business card. And made no sense. But not much of his undead life did right now, Ron thought, so he went with it.

"Yeah, all right. Ultrasound? Yous guys?"

Maria, clad only in a black lace bra, stirred atop the black granite island countertop. Clearly it was not the most comfortable place to be getting your jumbly bits sussed out like they were be-ing audited, and Maria had had enough. She sat up, hissed at Don Doctor, turned to Ron, and said one word.

"Brains!"

"I think we want the ultrasound, Doc Vito," Ron said. 'Brains' as a word between Maria and Ron seemed to be, to Ron's young ears – young only because he and Maria had been dating for such a short time and ears in a new relationship are young until the first fight – a word of agreement, of security, of understanding. Like calling your woman 'Snookums' or some shit. He looked over and Doc Vito was cowering in the corner, next to the new double door stainless steel refrigerator. What the fuck?

"What's up, doc?" Jim asked, and then snickered. "Did you take a wrong turn at Albuquerque?"

"She – she said brains," the doctor said, from his corner, where he looked like he had seen a ghost. Or a zombie.

"She said 'trains,' doc," Stella replied. "She's preparing for when my brother develops a Thomas the Tank Engine fetish. As boys do."

"Oh, yeah, my son likes those too. Sorry, I thought she was a zombie or something," the doc said, standing up very slowly.

"She might be, so you should hurry," Stella said, her eyebrows standing up like two overly enthusiastic students in a high school history class.

"Yeah," Ron said, "Hurry. You never when she'll need to eat actual brains. Like yours." Ron reached out and touched Doc Vito's head and playfully squeezed it. Vito shook.

"We're kidding, Doc," Stella said. "She's not a zombie. Obvi. She's having a baby. You said it yourself."

"Brains!" Maria shrieked from her position atop the countertop.

"Right, she's having a baby," the doctor said, his brow pearling with sweat. "Well, then, shall we get on with it?"

"We shall," Stella said, and winked at Ron. The doctor reached over and turned on his computer screen, which looked a lot like a Commodore 64, Ron realized. Surely they had better equipment these days than the machines that Ron used to play 'The Last Ninja' on back in the mid-80s, right? Then the doctor grabbed a wand looking thing and rubbed some grease all over Maria's belly.

"What's that, doc?"

"That is a transducer. It sends waves back to the computer, where we can see them."

"Like in the Rocky Horror Picture Show?"

Vito, Stella and Jim all turned to look at Ron like he had just yelled out that he had sex with his English teacher in the middle of a suddenly quiet English class.

"Whaaat?" Ron asked, innocently.

"Sorta like that, yeah," Vito finally answered, after what seemed like an inordinate amount of time of people staring at Ron like he was an idiot. He knew he was an idiot; he just didn't want word to spread.

Vito rubbed some Vasoline on Maria's belly and took his transducer, which made Ron giggle, because Rocky Horror Picture Show, and went to work. After about three and a half minutes of "uh huh"s and "right"s and "Oooh, that's interesting," he paused and turned to Ron, Jim and Stella, all watching intently.

"Do you want to know?"

All three of them looked at each other, and Ron finally spoke. "We already know."

"You do?" Vito asked.

"Yeah," Ron said.

"Your transducer is smaller than the transducer in the Rocky Horror Picture Show, but they do operate under similar technologies -"

"Of course we wanna fucking know," Stella shouted. "Am I going to have a brother or a sister?"

"Well," Vito said, pointing at the screen, "based on this rather large penis right here -"

"A BROTHER?" Stella shrieked. "YES! I'm gonna teach that fucker how to smoke, how to drink -"

"How to swear," Ron said, stating the obvious.

"How to eat people," Jim said, staring at the garbage disposal again.

"What?" Vito asked, preparing to cower in the corner again.

"How to uh, eat, uh, pie," Ron replied.

"Yes, we all LOVE pie," Stella exclaimed, covering for the zombies in the room one more time. She nudged Ron in the ribs with her elbow. "Don't we, fellas?"

"Apple and cherry and pumpkin and banana cream!" Ron exclaimed, licking his lips.

"And meat pie! And peop – ur, pecan pie!" Jim exclaimed, his eyes bulging as he stared at Vito's butt. Clearly he was hungry.

Vito took a step back. "Did he say people?"

"You did say it was a baby boy, right?" Stella asked.

"Yes," Doctor Vito replied.

"YES," Stella shrieked again and ran out of the room.

"BRAINS!" Maria shrieked from atop the granite countertop, her belly high in the air. She looked like she wanted to shuffle out of the house, like the zombie she was, but she was a pantsless zombie, and that would attract the wrong kind of attention.

CHAPTER
5

Ron – Zombie.
Maria – Pregnant zombie.
Stella – Teenager.
Jim – Zombie and lovin' it!
Watson Son – Gestating.

Las Vegas is known as the Gambling Capital of the World, Sin City, Lost Wages, The City That Never Sleeps, City of Lights, Fun Town…and the Entertainment Capital of the World. "Entertainment" being a very loose word. Sure, you can go see Celine Dion sing the 'Titanic' theme song or whatever in a giant casino arena with 4,297 other Dioniacs, and you can go see any of 187 Cirque Du Soleil Shows, and you can go see every Broadway musical that ever existed at any number of casino theaters, but you can also, should you choose to do so, stuff dollar bills down a 43-year-old stripper's tattered g-string, eat at the buffet at Circus Circus (and spend the next several days praying to your porcelain God), or go to the Bourbon Room to see a cheesy Elvis impersonator show featuring five different Elvises.

The Bourbon Room was a dark nightclub on the floor of Venetian that catered to a bit of an older crowd. Late nights, it played videos from the early days of MTV (yes, kids, they used to actually play videos!) and encouraged the gathered middle-aged crowd to get drunk enough to find each other attractive. Earlier on Thursday, Friday and Saturday evenings, Bourbon Room hosted a Five Elvis Show, featuring Portly Elvis, Mexican Elvis, Midget Elvis, Skinny Elvis, and Captain Elvis. It was, in their words, "the only fucking Elvis show anywhere with five different Elvises!" Only in Vegas, right?

The Bourbon Room on this Friday night was even busier than it was on Thursday night, and Portly Elvis was happy about that. It meant more Mai-tais and more women for him, both of which he enjoyed, obviously. He waltzed in the side door and ran into Sidney, a gorgeous 26-year-old redhead cocktail waitress/yoga instructor (today she was a redhead; sometimes she was a blonde; nobody who works in the Vegas service industry has their natural hair color anymore) whom PE had the hots for. Well, it was more than that. They dated at one point, until PE couldn't keep Little Elvis in his pants and cheated on her with a video poker party pit dancer at Bally's named Sidney (Portly Elvis claimed he was confused by the name), and Sidney unceremoniously dumped him. Literally. There was no ceremony at all…unless you count Sidney crying a lot a 'ceremony.' He smirked; he still had the hots for her after all these months and she seemed to have the hots for him (or maybe that was all in his imagination; PE did have a very active imagination) but Portly Elvis also knew that when a cheater re-wants his cheatee, that cheater is so far down the cheatee's man-chart that she would probably never give him a second chance. It was a lesson he never learned, more than once.

Sidney looked at PE and winced. "What the fuck are you doing here, David? We heard you weren't coming in today! And," Sidney's cheeks puffed out like she wanted to puke, "did somebody die?" Sidney was the only person in Las Vegas who knew that PE's real name was 'David;' he told her one night in that post-mutual-orgasm fog of honesty when every hidden truth is in danger of slipping out.

'What? Do I look bad, Sid?' is how Portly Elvis' brain replied, but his mouth? His mouth was living in a different country, speaking a foreign language, one that Portly Elvis was wholly unfamiliar with. "Braaaaaaiiiiiiins" is what his mouth said. What the fuck?

"You fucking reek! Oh my fucking God!" Sidney closed her nostrils with the fingers of her right hand while balancing a tray of drinks with her left hand. "Fuck, David!" She strode rapidly away.

PE took a whiff. Sure, he could have used some deodorant, but he didn't smell THAT bad. He went to the bar to get a Mai-tai. One was on the house, and PE always liked to have his before the show started. It helped calm his nerves and slip into his Elvis character. If you've ever tried the Elvis accent, it's easier if you're a little tipsy. It's a bit of a slur anyway, and it usually came out something like. *uhhhhh......thankyouverymuchmommababy.....*

Crystal, the bartender at Bourbon Room, had her head down behind the bar as PE approached. "Brrraaaa -"

RAAAAAAALPH. Uh oh, PE thought, Crystal was sick. She wasn't going to be any good to anybody tonight.

She lifted her head, her blonde hair askew, her face ashen. "What the fuck is that smell, Portly?" She covered her mouth with her right hand. "Oh, fuck, it's you!"

And puked again into a trash can behind the bar.

Athena, a beautiful mixed race cocktail waitress with an incredible Afro, walked over, her right hand fingers on her nose, her left hand handing PE a bottle of cologne. "Here, Porthly," she said, with that funny nasally accent that happens when you talk with your nose plugged, "Put thith on before you make uth *all* puke."

PE took the bottle and looked at it. 'Eau D' Zombie.' Really? He opened it as Sidney came back by and flipped him off with her right hand. "Ooooh sthink, thucker," she yelled. PE took a whiff of the bottle...and it smelled like every other cologne he'd ever smelled. That is to say, a hint of wood, failure, and broken dreams. He splashed some on his face as Crystal puked behind the bar again and Athena shot lasers at him with her eyes. Not literally, because even in this story that would be insane, but figuratively. Damn, PE thought, I must really stink. Usually when he walked into Bourbon Room before a show Sid, Crystal and Athena were all fun and games and laughs. But tonight they were all ready to kill him. Or puke.

He walked around back to the bathroom, took off his polyester Elvis shirt, and looked in the mirror. He looked good, damn. Like somebody had cleaned him up and put foundation on his face. Elvis was a guy and wasn't totally familiar with makeup, but he was also a Vegas performer so he knew enough about it to be dangerous. Or stupid. Or dangerously stupid.

Anyway, whoever had applied the foundation had done a fantastic job. And his hair was amazing! Jet black – no gray! – and coiffed in perfect Elvis style. Who did this?

In the Bourbon Room, Ron and Jim, dressed in their matching white velour track suits – they had taken to calling themselves 'brofessional track stars' – said hi to Crystal, Sidney and Athena, old friends from their days as Vegas humans. They procured a couple of bourbons, neat, and took seats in the back of the room, in the dark so nobody would recognize Ron. He was still in a bit of shock from hearing the news that he was having a human baby boy, so he and Jim were taking a boys night out. Without paparazzi, hopefully.

"Ladies and Gentlemen," Portly Elvis heard Marky Mark, the Bourbon Room MC, from the stage, "Welcome to the Bourbon Room and the best fucking Elvis show on the Strip – the only fucking Elvis show anywhere with five different Elvises!"

Oh, shit, PE thought, the show was about to start. As the crowd went wild out in the Bourbon Room, he doused himself with Eau D' Zombie, threw his shirt on, and went out to get in line with Mexican, Midget, Skinny and Captain Elvis. He eyed each one of them suspiciously as he said hi to each one with a head nod. They, in turn, winced as their olfactory senses went bananas at the smell of an entire bottle of zombie cologne on his body. PE took their winces not as signs of destruction of their nasal cavities but as acknowledgment that they were the fuckers who pranked him last night.

And unbeknownst to Mexican Elvis, Midget Elvis, Skinny Elvis, and Captain Elvis, it was the last wince Mexican Elvis, Midget Elvis, Skinny Elvis, and Captain Elvis would ever make.

"Ladies and Gentlemen, Skinny Elvis!" Skinny Elvis careened onto the stage like a bumper car driven by a fetus. It was his shtick; he was the out-of-control Elvis, always moving fast, always going crazy. It's what made him skinny. Well, that and the fact that all he ate was bourbon. And all he drank was speed.

"And Midget Elvis!" The Bourbon Room crowd cheered; Midget Elvis was a fan favorite. You'd be surprised how many women want to bang a midget. He strode on stage with his short gait, because he was a midget, and his gleaming smile, because he knew how many women want to bang a midget. Little dude knew how to work a room…and how to get into a woman's pants.

"And Captain Elvis!" The Bourbon Room cheered a little louder. Midget was a fan favorite, for sure, but nobody ever knew what Captain Elvis was going to do. He was a stand-up comic on his non-Elvis nights, so he had an amazing sense of humor, and he brought that with him to the Bourbon Room. Many nights he would go out into the crowd and loudly try to find a woman to be the Tennille to his Captain, a woman who wanted some of his Muskrat Love. You'd be surprised how many women want to bang a muskrat. Or a captain.

"Senoras y senoras, damas y caballeros, ninos y ninas…les presento, para su placer las noches, Mexican Elvis!" The Bourbon Room went crazy. Mex (it's what his Elvis friends called him) came on in his Elvis jumpsuit covered in a sarape, an oversized sombrero on his head, riding a tiny man dressed like a bull. The whole thing was quite racist, really, but Mex quickly ditched the racist elements of his act once he crossed the Bourbon Room floor and took his place in the lineup on stage. But not before he played up his matador angle and pretended to fight and defeat the tiny man dressed like a bull. Vegas shtick at its worst. Or best, depending on who was watching. And how much they'd had to drink.

"And finally," Marky Mark, a middle aged man with a shirt open to his waist and a blonde frohawk wig atop his head, began rousing the crowd up for the headliner of the evening. "The only Elvis in the world big enough for the Vegas Strip! The only Elvis in the world who can eat the entire Venetian buffet for breakfast, the Caesar's Palace buffet for lunch, and your mom for dinner." PE did a few stretches to get ready. Well, they weren't 'stretches' per se, because PE was so fat he really couldn't stretch, they were more like thoughts of stretches, images of stretches….okay, fuck it, he took a few breaths. And Marky Mark kept going. "The only Elvis in the world big enough to have his own Graceland in his pants – we call it 'Waistband' – ladies and gentlemen, boys and girls, chicks and dudes, give it up for Portllllllly Elvis!"

PE waltzed across the dance floor of the Bourbon Room, blowing kisses to Sidney, Crystal, Athena, and the gathered crowd of mid-western and coastal tourists, his hips moving so that his belly jiggled purposefully, falling out of his unbuttoned-to-the-waist jumpsuit on purpose, dancing like a jello tower in a windstorm. The crowd always loved that part of his dance; PE wasn't sure if they were cheering or jeering, but he knew that any reaction was a good reaction, so fuck it.

And then, as he danced, he smelled something that made him hungry. He pointed his nose towards the smell. Was it the fresh tacos that Rosa made every hour at the Venetian Food Court? No, his nose wanted to go a different direction. He swiveled; was it the high end steak place over in Restaurant Row? That place probably smelled good, but no. He swiveled again.

The smell came from the stage.

Portly Elvis lifted his head slightly and looked at the stage. Skinny, Captain, Midget and Mex were there, dancing their particular dances. Skinny like a meth addict, Captain like a 1970s porn star, Midget like a small man with a huge cock, and Mex like a caballero. No food to be seen, anywhere.

Or was there?

PE headed towards his usual Bourbon Room place, onstage, in the middle, between Captain Elvis and Mexican Elvis. He started doing his dance, which was a takeoff of Pee-Wee Herman's "Tequila" dance as done by a large man. Portly Elvis could do it in his sleep, which was good, because at the moment he was focused not on the dance but on finding the food that his nose knew was close by. Portly Elvis had hyperosmia, his doctor said, which was a heightened sense of smell, but PE always thought that his large stomach needed so much food that his olfactory senses grew to accommodate it. No hyperwhatever bullshit necessary. And at the moment, his hyperosmia – if that's what it was – was telling him that the food was on stage with him.

His stomach growled and he reached down to pat it, like a pet, and accidentally scratched off a flap of skin.

What the fuck?

Captain Elvis danced close to PE during his 'somebody has to pay for this pizza' porn star bit, and Portly's head whipped around to his left as his nostrils burned with desire.

Captain Elvis was the food.

Portly Elvis' belly took over and he licked his lips, opened his mouth, and took a bite out of Captain Elvis' neck. And had an orgasm. Nothing, in his 42 years of life, had ever tasted as good, and PE had eaten at every restaurant in Las Vegas and some in Reno, so he knew what was good. Captain tasted like a perfectly done medium-rare steak at the high end steak place in Restaurant Row, with the melt-in-your-mouth quality that only high-end steak places could pull off with regularity.

Blood spurted out of Captain Elvis' neck as he fell to the floor and the music stopped. Portly Elvis smelled a buffet to his right and his head whipped around that direction and came face to face with Mexican Elvis, who looked like he had just seen a friend take a bite out of another friend. Mex smelled as delicious as the creme brulee at the Caesar's Palace buffet, Portly Elvis' favorite dessert in the entire world, so he took a bite of Mex's face and came again and the Bourbon Room started screaming. Okay, not the Bourbon Room itself, because that would be weird, but the people in Bourbon Room. All of them. Screaming at once.

It might have been the blood spurting out of Mex's face. Or it might have been Mex's body falling limp to the floor.

Or it might have been Portly Elvis taking a bite out of Marky Mark's ass. It rather tasted like salty pork loin, PE decided, as the tourists began running out of the Bourbon Room into the Venetian casino, trying to escape the horrific scene that was PE and his snacks inside the Bourbon Room.

Tourists. Screaming.

It was the sound of the end of mankind.

A face appeared in his view, a face that he remembered from souvenirs around town. A famous face. He stopped eating Marky Mark's ass long enough for Marky Mark to slump to the floor, dead.

"STOP," Ron Watson shrieked, holding Portly Elvis by the neck. "You can't eat these people, they don't fucking deserve it!"

"BRAAIIIIIIINNNNNNNNNS" Portly Elvis screamed as Jim tackled him to the dance floor in the Bourbon Room, blood splashing up into the air, polk-a-dotting Ron's white velour tracksuit. Portly Elvis' head found itself surrounded by a trio of gun barrels quicker than you could say 'Tequila.' Guns held by Sidney, Athena and Crystal.

"Fuck, David, what are you doing?" Sidney's face was angry, yet sad, and maybe just a little annoyed. Portly Elvis remembered that face from the night she had figured out he had fucked Sydney, the video poker party pit dancer at Bally's. And yeah, he had fucked her. Every which way from here to a full house to three of a kind to a royal flush.

"Yeah, Portly, what's up?" Athena's face was angry bewilderment. And no, he had never seen that face before.

"Do we have to cap your ass?" Crystal asked, adopting the spirit of an LA street gangsta, even though she was a blonde woman in her mid-20s in Las Vegas. She was still holding a gun to PE's head, and she was holding it sideways, like a gangsta. PE decided she must have grown up in LA. Or watched a lot of 'Cops.'

"Brains," PE said, and that's all he could say. "BRAINS." In an Elvis accent.

Athena turned to look at Crystal and Sidney. "He's a fucking zombie."

Sidney's angry/sad/annoyed face melted and tears rolled like the end credits on a bad movie. "He's a ZOMBIE?" Her gun dug deeper into PE's skull.

"He is," Ron said. "I would know."

"BRAINS," PE said in his defense, even though he was trying to say something more like, 'hey, ladies, I don't know how I got this way, I woke up this morning in a box and now, hey, look, here we are. Look at the time! I gotta go.'

But no, it came out "BRAINS."

Crystal looked at her friends and pushed the gun further into PE's temple. "We gotta kill his zombie ass, yo. Cap his ass."

PE looked at Sidney, who was sobbing, and the ground at the dead Elvi and Marky Mark; they were all stirring, slowly, like sleepy teenagers on the first day of school. Shit, Ron thought, they were about to become zombies.

"We can't kill him," Sidney said to Crystal. "We can't cap his ass. I still -"

"Yes we fucking can," Athena interrupt, her Afro shining under the lights of the darkened club. She looked like she was wearing a halo, even as she prepared to shoot Portly Elvis in the head.

"You have to shoot him in the head," Ron said, trying to clean blood off of himself with a bar towel. And that's when Portly Elvis hit him square in the jaw. Portly was fat, but he was also strong, and Ron went down as fast and easy as a pornstar after the word 'action,' his body sprawled out on the bloody Bourbon Room floor.

"FUCK. YOU." Portly Elvis said, and that's when Jim hit him square in the jaw. Jim was skinny, but he was also strong, and Portly Elvis went down as fast and easy as a presidential candidate's polling numbers after he says he can grab women by the pussy.

"No, fuck YOU," Jim said, standing over Portly Elvis' prone rotund body like a prizefighter who had just knocked out his opponent 17 seconds into the first round.

"NO," Sidney screamed, tears streaming down her cheek, her red hair glowing under the nightclub lights, her gun now pointed at Jim. "I'm not gonna – It wasn't -"

"Wasn't what," Crystal replied.

"Wasn't his f-f-f-fault." Sidney's whole face sobbed, like it was putting on a sobbing show. If this were a circus, her sobs would have been in the Big Top.

"You still fucking love him, don't you?" Athena asked, her Bourbon Room tank top revealing her smooth shoulders under the disco ball of the club. PE had a thing for shoulders. Sidney must have, too, because she was pointing her gun at Athena's shoulders.

"Fuck," Crystal said, "You still love that fucker? Even after he just ate all his competition?"

"And made a mess of the Bourbon Room?" Athena asked.

Ron looked around. Yeah, this was kind of a mess. It looked like one of his hotel rooms after he dined.

Portly Elvis lifted himself off of the bloody floor of the Bourbon Room, his white jumpsuit now a pinkish color, and tried to explain what was going on, even though he himself wasn't sure. This did seem like a good time to butt into the conversation, though.

"BRAINS," he said. Fuck. His vocabulary was as short as his penis.

"We have to let him go," Sidney said to Crystal and Athena through her tears. "He didn't mean it."

"Brains," Portly Elvis said again, which this time meant, 'Yeah, I didn't mean it. They just smelled SO good!'

"He's a zombie," Ron said. Not only was Portly Elvis a zombie, he thought, he was a bad zombie. And not even a kind bad zombie, the kind who apologized before eating a human being. Ron had a met a few of those in his time, and they were his friends. Portly Elvis, however, was not that at all and could never be Ron's friend, only his enemy. First rule of Ron's zombie friend club is you never talk about Ron's zombie friend club. Second rule is be fucking nice to your food. We're all in this together.

"HE'S A FUCKING ZOMBIE," Athena said as Sidney pushed the gun into her face.

"OKAY!" Crystal replied, concerned for both of her friends. 'OKAY' is usually the first word you say when one of your best friends is being threatened by a gun held by another of your best friends, scientific studies show. It really is the universal keeping-the-peace first-thing-you-think-of kind of word. She reached up and moved the gun slowly down from Athena's face. She then dropped her own gun down to her waist. "He can go. But he better go now, before security gets here."

"You heard her," Sidney said, as she sidled up to Portly Elvis and kissed his zombie face. "You should go." Her sad puppy-dog eyes raised and for a moment she had the saddest face in the history of the mankind. She then brightened up and made the international sign for *call me*, placing her phone-shaped hand against her face.

"Brains," PE replied, even as in his mind he was saying, 'Thanks, babe, I *will* call you,' and he shuffled out of Bourbon Room towards the Las Vegas Strip.

Ron and Jim stood with their three friends in the bloody Bourbon Room and wondered what the fuck just happened.

CHAPTER

6

Ron – Zombie.
Maria – Pregnant zombie.
Stella – Teenager.
Jim – Zombie and lovin' it!
Watson Son – Gestating.

As children, many of us are taught that in order to be successful in life, we need to go to college, get a degree, and start in a career that will last until we retire at 65 or 85 or whenever-the-fuck-we-can-afford-to-retire. And many of us do just that. Get on the corporate ladder, get on the fast track, and work until we're dead…or whenever-the-fuck-we-can-afford-to-retire.

But many of us, at the age of 18, don't know what the hell we really want to do with our lives. However, we're told this is the path to success, so we go to college and we study something – anything, really – and we get a degree in something – anything, really – and we go to work in that field and, at some point, years down the line, we realize that that field isn't what our heart truly desires and that that career isn't what our soul was designed to do. In other words, we picked the wrong fucking major.

Ron Watson was a zombie. He knew that now, after reading his own obituary and seeing what happened at the Bourbon Room the other night. When Portly Elvis starting chomping on people like they were a fancy brunch, Ron jumped in to help stop him, but he got it. He understood that feeling of being hungry and of knowing that only human flesh and blood could sate that hunger. It wasn't what his heart truly desired or what his soul was designed to do, but Zombie was his major. His wrong fucking major. He *was* a zombie, and he wasn't at all happy about it. And where does a man or a zombie go when he's not at all happy about something? He goes to the bar.

Carnaval Court, Ron and Jim's favorite circular outdoor bar between Harrah's and Imperial Palace/The Quad/The Linq/whateverthefucktheywerecallingitnow – well, actually, it was the *only* circular outdoor bar between Harrah's and Imperial Palace/The Quad/The Linq/whateverthefucktheywerecallingitnow, but it was Ron and Jim's favorite bar in the world – was, on this Monday, a bit slower than normal, so everybody had to work a little harder to make their tips. Vache, today's bartender, was putting an extra couple of turns on his bottles as they went into the air. Tony, the guitarist for The Whipits, the 1980s house band, was playing his guitar with his tongue, and Robin, the singer for The Whipits, was dancing on the bartop singing Heart's "Barracuda," one of Ron's favorite songs. Dazzling in a skimpy black tank top, tight black pants, and knee-high black pleather boots, with her platinum blonde pixie hair cut and an authentic black S & M whip by her side, she looked like she would be the sexiest character in *The Rocky Horror Picture Show*.

Ron wandered into Carnaval Court, his head in his hands (figuratively), his soul on the ground (also figuratively). He needed a drink and he needed time to think. What he didn't need was to get his ass whipped by Robin, and when she tried to do just that, he glared at her like she was from Planet Motherfucker.

"Damn, Ron, chill," Robin said. "Having a bad day?"

"You could say that," Ron replied. "I'm a zombie."

"We know, bitch!" Robin said. "Do you think that was a secret? Barracuda!" Yes, the song was still going, with Tony playing solos like he was Jimmy Page's brother, and Robin singing like she was Ann Wilson in the 1970s.

"Sell me sell you, the porpoise said, dive down deep to save my head…" She leaned back whilst standing on the bartop and her supple neck shone in the bright Las Vegas sun, a brief bright spot in Ron's black day. A woman's neck was sexy and no matter how zombie Ron was, he still admired sexy, even on a human.

"What are you drinkin', Ron?" Vache was his usual bouncy, crazy self, which Ron wasn't really in the mood for, but what the hell. He knew Vache was making an assumption about his own mood, based on the general mood of the place, which was almost always, "Hey, we're in Vegas, let's party," and Ron wasn't going to hold that against him.

"Bourbon. Please." Ron's stomach rumbled lightly, like the start of a hot rod race for pink slips.

"Ooh, movin' up in the world. Bourbon, coming right up! You want some antidote with that?" Ron laughed as Vache grabbed a bottle of the Elmer T. Lee Bourbon (only the best for regulars!) and threw it in the air, a plastic cup following along like a younger brother emulating his older sibling. Both landed in Vache's hands, and a cup of Elmer T Bourbon appeared in front of Ron faster than you can say 'alcoholic.'

"Bour-Bon for my boy-Ron," Vache exclaimed in his loudest voice, drowning out the final verse of "Barracuda" as Robin danced around the circular bartop, whipping tourists' asses with her whip. In spite of his mood, Ron still loved this place.

But his mood? That was something different. Fuck, I'm a fucking zombie, Ron thought. I guess I always thought I had a chance to go back, but after seeing my obituary and relating to Zombie Elvis, there was no chance. It was as defined – I'm dead. I'm a zombie. I ain't coming back from that. I graduated with the wrong fucking major. The realization had hit him this morning about as hard as the semi truck had hit him back in Colorado. Sometimes bad realizations have a way of laying in wait and springing up when and where you least expect it, like a rattlesnake on a paved city running trail.

He took a swig of his bourbon; it went down smooth and oak-ey, like a smooth and oak-ey hooker. Okay, not really. It was more like tree sap that had been warmed up over a campfire for five minutes.

"Is that good?" A sexy voice to Ron's left. He swiveled in his plastic barstool. A brunette was sitting next to him; a beautiful brunette with shoulder length hair, bangin' body, black tank top, blue jeans, and bright red lipstick.

"What?"

"The Elmer T."

"Oh, yeah, it's great." Ron took a swig. "It goes down smooth and oak-ey, like a smooth and oak-ey hooker. Or like tree sap that has been warmed up over a campfire for five minutes. Depending on how your day's going."

The brunette laughed. "You're funny."

"Thanks," Ron said…and then his stomach gurgled, like Mount St. Helens on eruption day. Fuck, he was hungry.

"Vache, I'll take a smooth and oak-ey hooker." The brunette was ordering herself a drink. And Ron's stomach wished it was eating.

"One Elmer T, coming right up." Bottles and cups flew in the air, a quiet cacophony above Vache's head existing in chaos until everything landed perfectly in Vache's hands and a cup of Elmer T. Lee bourbon appeared in front of the brunette, seemingly placed there by an invisible hand.

The brunette took a sip of her bourbon, stuck her hand out, and introduced herself. "I'm Joey."

Ron's stomach growled and stuck his own hand out. "I'm R -"

"I know who you are. I'm a fan." The brunette pulled the sleeve of her shirt aside to reveal a 'Brah' bra strap.

"Wow, you *are* a fan. Wait, Joey? Like you're one of the Ramones?"

"My mom and dad were big fans, so, yeah. That's exactly right. They had already used Johnny and Tommy on my brothers and Dee Dee on my sister, so I got Joey."

The brunette laughed and Ron's stomach growled again...and all of a sudden he was talking to a ham. Not just any ham, either, this was a big, thick slice of spiral-cut Honeybaked Ham. Holy fuck.

"I think they hoped I was going to be a boy," the ham said, speaking out of its perfectly circular bone in the middle of its perfectly circular pink slice of pig shank. Ron felt his mouth drool a tiny bit. And his nostrils...well, they smelled deliciously roasted ham, with a hint of brown sugar and maple. He closed his eyes and lifted his nose in the air, like a puppy smelling for a squirrel. Yep, that was ham. It was a smell that, as good smells often do, led Ron to a compliment. He closed his eyes and lifted his nose in the air, again like a puppy smelling for a squirrel.

"You smell good, ham."

"Thanks. Wait, what?"

"Joey. You smell...good...Joey." Ron's stomach growled again, and all of a sudden he was talking to a pot pie. Not just any pot pie, either, this was a chicken pot pie, inside a ceramic bowl, filled with the best vegetables from the best vegetable gardens and the best free-range organic chicken pieces from the best free-range organic chicken piece farms and topped with the flakiest crust from the best flaky crust bakeries. It was a five-star pot pie, according to Ron's nostrils. And Ron's nostrils were never wrong. Especially when it came to pot pies.

"Thanks, Ron," said the pot pie, speaking out of the tiny hole created in the middle of the crust to let the steam out. Ron had never seen a pot pie speak before, but this was how he always imagined it would go. Words coming out of the steam hole, the rest of the crust wrinkling up to go with the words, like the face of a 70-year-old man telling stories about his grandkids.

"I secretly always wished my parents had been big fans of KISS," the pot pie said, steam coming out of its hole along with the words. "Then maybe my name could have been Jean." When the word *Jean* and its accompanying smells hit Ron in the face, he could hold back no longer. He leaned over to the pot pie, stuck his nose in her neck, and inhaled.

"You smell *delicious*, pot pie. *DE. LISH. US.*"

The pot pie giggled and Ron's stomach growled again and all of a sudden he was talking to a brisket. Then a new york strip steak. Then a grilled ribeye. Then carnitas tacos. Ron took his face out of Joey's neck, stood up, and backed away from the bar. His stomach growled and she was a filet mignon. WHAT. THE. FUCK!

"You okay?" the filet mignon asked, its bacon being held tightly against its beef with a toothpick. Ron knew the answer to the question; no, he wasn't okay. No, he was hungry as fuck and Joey, the brunette, was also a ham, a pot pie, a brisket, a New York strip steak, a ribeye, tacos, and a filet mignon. He had to eat her. But he couldn't; as far as he knew, she was guilty of nothing more than sitting down next to him at Carnaval Court and chatting him up. Certainly not an eatable offense, according to Ron's set of morals and standards. But he was SO HUNNNNNNGGGGGGRY! Fuck it, he thought, he was a zombie now, and why the fuck should he worry about his own set of morals and standards? Those things came in handy when he thought there was a chance he could be human again someday, but now that he knew that was impossible? Time to start acting like a fucking zombie. Like all those other fucking zombies who could fucking eat whoever they could catch and not fucking worry about whether or not somebody deserved it. Fuck morals. Fuck standards. Fuck hunger.

"I'm okay, Joey. Sorry, it's been a week."

"It's okay," she replied, with a sultry voice that might have been better suited to a naked Saturday morning in bed, with fresh coffee and muffins, then to a clothed Monday about-to-be-eaten-by-a-zombie afternoon.

"I would have named you Jean."

"You are funny!" She nuzzled her face into his neck, repaying the gesture he had made earlier when she was a pot pie. He knew she was going to be his next meal, but if she wanted to nuzzle, he wasn't going to stop her. He was a zombie now, none of those bullshit human rules applied to him anymore.

"You wanna get out of here, Jean?" Ron stroked her silk black hair with his zombie hand; the contrast between the two was stark, like life and death. And soon his life was going to be her death, Ron thought, as his stomach prepared to fill with scrumptious human pulp...and her death was going to be his life.

"Yeah, Ron. Let's go back to my room at the Venetian." She raised her face to kiss him and he felt a longing in his black soul, a yearning to return to his primordial state, his state of automaton, where he ate mechanically, anyone was a meal, it didn't matter, and his loins animated and his groin awakened and his pelvis vibrated and...actually, that was his phone in his jeans vibrating. He gave Joey the "hold on" signal – one finger in the air – and pulled out his phone. On it was a text message from Stella.

"Time to go to the hospital; your ho is having your baby and you're going to be a Daddy! Again! Hope you do better with this one! I'M PARKED ON THE CURB, ASSHOLE, HURRY!"

CHAPTER
7

Ron – Zombie.
Maria – Dilated five cm.
Stella – Teenager.
Jim – Zombie and lovin' it!
Watson Son – Loading.

Carnaval Court has no parking, as it is sandwiched between hotels and right on the Las Vegas Strip, but that didn't stop Stella from putting two wheels of her El Camino up on the concrete curb dividing the street and the sidewalk and, via her middle finger, introducing the bird to everybody who drove by on the street or walked by on the sidewalk. It had dawned on her that she was about to become a big sister and it had also dawned on her that that meant she had the sole responsibility to introduce her younger brother to the joys of a perfect life (whiskey, cigarettes, muscle cars, and dealing with your zombie dad), so she didn't give a shit who she pissed off, because this was going to be epic fun.

Except maybe she shouldn't have pissed off the two cops who had showed up, via Segways, next to the half-on-the-curb-half-on-the-street El Camino. Sure, a city like Las Vegas couldn't pay cops very well, but they could buy them Segways. This made no sense to Stella, but she figured somebody had naked pictures of some politician or city budget person with a goat or something, 'cuz that's how illogical back room deals that led to every cop having a Segway were made, in her mind.

"You stupid motherfuckers, my dad needs to go the hospital right now because his slut is about to give birth and I'm about to become a big sister!" Stella, who was dressed in black leather shorts, a white tank top, black fishnet leggings and black Doc Marten boots, obviously wore her heart on her sleeve.

Except, since she was wearing a tank top, she didn't have a sleeve… so the policemen didn't see her heart and weren't buying her story. And, of course, they were staring at her chest. Because tank top!

"Young lady, you're causing a traffic jam all the way back to Luxor. You need to move this rustbucket NOW," said Cop #1, who, in a strange fit of stereotyping, looked a lot like Jon Baker from the TV show CHiPs. Albeit an overweight Jon Baker. Blonde hair, matching black shorts and shirt (short-sleeve, to accommodate the weather), black belt, black shoes, flesh colored hump where his six pack should have been. Yes, it was visible; Fat Jon wasn't a stickler for getting all his buttons fastened, apparently. And it was more than a hump; if Fat Jon had been pregnant it most certainly would have produced quintuplets. Or more.

Ron made his way to the El Camino from Carnaval Court, after letting his food – ur, Jean – ur, JOEY – stay – a decision he regretted from one part of his anatomy, at least – and looked at Jon's partner. Sure enough, he could have been a Madame Tussaud's Wax Museum stand-in for Ponch Poncherello. From CHiPs. Dark hair, brown skin, same outfit as Jon, and a look on his face that said "I'll be your best friend and bang your wife behind your back" and a look on his paunch (Ron wondered if that's where he got his name) that said, "Not really; I'm too fat for even your wife." Ron wondered, for a brief moment, if anybody gave enough of a shit about Ponch or Jon anymore to warrant them having a wax figure at a wax figure place. He made a mental note to walk over to Madame Tussaud's at the Venetian sometime to find out. He also made a mental note to wonder why fat cops needed Segways. Shouldn't they be walking? For their health? And how fast could a Segway move anyway? If one of those cops ended up on the TV show "Cops" chasing a shirtless man between endless rows of mobile homes, would they ever catch him? Ron thought not and giggled to himself. He might have giggled out loud but everybody knows you don't do that in front of cops. Just like everybody knows you don't talk back to cops.

Almost everybody. "She's not a rustbucket, you hippopotamic land mass," Stella said, "she's a 1968 El Camino SS with 375 horses under her hood!" She was looking at Fat Ponch like a middle school math teacher looks at a student who claims that the area of a circle is base times height. There was more disdain in her glare than in all the Catholic schools in the country at that moment.

"Wait, wait, wait. Did she just -" Fat Ponch looked at Fat Jon.

"Did she?" Fat Jon's mouth fell open. He looked at Stella, as a Ferrari passed by and yelled 'Get that fucking rustbucket off of the street!' Well, it probably wasn't the Ferrari yelling, it was probably the occupants, but still.

"Did I what?" Stella asked.

"Did you just quote the Princess Bride?" Fat Ponch asked.

"It's possible, pigs."

"She did it again!" Fat Jon said.

"I might be bluffing. It's conceivable, you miserable, vomitous mass."

Fat Ponch giggled. "I LOVE that movie!"

"Do some more," Fat Jon said. "First things first, to the death."

"No," Stella said, quoting her favorite movie of all time. "To the pain."

"I don't think I'm quite familiar with that phrase," Fat Ponch said, winking at Fat Jon.

"I'll explain and I'll use small words so that you'll be sure to understand," Stella replied, in a stilted English accent. "You warthog faced buffoon. "

Fat Jon laughed. "That may be the first time in my life a man has dared insult me."

Stella smiled. "It won't be the last. To the pain means the first thing you will lose will be your feet below the ankles. Then your hands at the wrists. Next your nose."

Fat Jon and Fat Ponch spoke the next line in unison. "And then my tongue I suppose, I killed you too quickly the last time. A mistake I don't mean to duplicate tonight." They both laughed, overflowing bellies shaking in unison, like a couple of water balloons at an elementary school field day.

"I wasn't finished," Stella gleamed, "the next thing you will lose will be your left eye followed by your right -"

Ron, an incredulous look plastered on his face, interrupted the lovely geeky Princess Bride scene retelling because, frankly, he had more important shit to worry about at the moment. Besides, everybody knows that Westley was bluffing.

"I gotta get to the hospital, boys. Sorry about the rustbucket on the curb."

"DAD!"

"It *could* use a paint job."

"Hey, aren't you -" Fat Ponch looked at Fat Jon.

"Yeah, aren't you that guy, famous for that thing, you know..." Fat Jon was shaking his head and waving his hands through the air like a six-month old baby girl trying to explain the Theory of Relativity to her parents.

"You're Rob Zombie! That's it!" Fat Ponch's mouth fell open like a gumball dispenser at an amusement park. "I LOVE your movies, too!"

"I'm Ron Wats -" Ron paused. He was very hungry and he really needed to get to the hospital and did he give a fuck if these two fat fucks knew who he was? Not really. Sometimes you have to let shit go for the greater good, right? And right now his greater good was at the hospital, coming out of his zombie girlfriend's vagina. "Zombie. Rob Zombie. Exactly. Why the fuck not?"

"I love your music," Fat Jon said. "Will you sing one of your songs?"

"I really gotta get to the -"

"We won't cite your daughter," Fat Ponch said, "if you sing one of your songs."

"That's a savings of at least $500," Fat Jon said. "Parking on the Vegas curb ain't cheap."

"Ain't cheap, Mister Zombie," Fat Ponch echoed, like a parrot in severe need of a cracker.

Oh, fucking great, Ron thought. Now I'm Rob Fuckin' Zombie, singing a song to get my first daughter out of a ticket and to get me to the hospital so I can see my first son emerge from a zombie vagina. This was some fucked-up parenting shit right here.

"Oh, alright. Stella, get in the fucking rustbucket and drive. I'll sing as we're leaving."

"She's not a fucking rustbucket, dad!"

"Whatever. Drive."

The Fat CHIPS looked at each other and at Ron as Stella got into the driver seat, almost getting run over by a Lamborghini in the process. "Aaaaaaaaaaasshole," she yelled as the car passed her within inches of her hip.

"Well, Ron Zombie? You gonna sing?" Fat Jon asked. "Or do we give you and your daughter an eight-hundred dollar ticket?"

"I thought it was five hundred?"

"Price is going up," Fat Ponch joined in, a smirk on his face, "unless you sing!"

Stella started the El Camino up and shifted it into drive, as Ron climbed into the passenger seat and rolled the window down. "Okay, boys, here you go." He sang the only Rob Zombie song he knew, 'Thunder Kiss '65,' by White Zombie. "'NINETEEN SIXTY FIIIIIIIIIIIIVE, YEAH!"

Fat Jon and Fat Ponch both started dancing like drunk strippers and joined in singing as the El Camino pulled into Vegas Strip traffic. "FIIIIIIIIIIIIIVE, YEAH!" Ron sang the song just long enough to make sure the car was off the curb and stuck in traffic... which, being that it was the Las Vegas Strip, was not entirely unexpected. In fact, isn't 'not entirely unexpected' just a fancy-ass way of saying 'was totally expected?' Which, being that it was the Las Vegas Strip, it was. Traffic, that is. Totally expected, that is.

As the El Camino slowly creeped up the Las Vegas Strip towards the next intersection, which would take them to Vegas Valley View Memorial Medical Center (VVVMMC) and Ron's greater good, Stella reached down with her left hand and pulled up a pack of Marlboro Lights. With her right hand she pushed the cigarette lighter in to the dash of the El Camino...which meant that she had no hands on the steering wheel.

"HONEY!" Ron yelled as he grabbed the vinyl-clad steering wheel with his left hand and steered it back into his own lane, narrowly avoiding hitting the Maserati in the lane next to them.

"What the fuck, dad? I got it."

"No you don't!" Ron steered the El Camino to a stop just behind an Audi that had stopped in front of them. He fucking loved fucking Vegas fucking traffic. Actually, he had never driven in fucking Vegas fucking traffic before because he never had had a fucking car there before (yay taxis!), but he had sat in fucking Vegas fucking traffic in a fucking cab before...and he fucking hated fucking Vegas traffic.

"I'm steering with my fucking knee, dad." Stella pointed to her knee with her unlit cigarette; sure, it was touching the steering wheel, but was she really *steering* with it? Ron's mother used to do that all the time when he was a kid...from grandmother to granddaughter, right?

The cigarette lighter popped out and Stella raised it to light her cigarette, her knee still on the steering wheel. Ron took a deep breath and, with his hand, let go of the steering wheel. At some point you gotta trust your first daughter a little bit, right?

Stella lit her cigarette and put the lighter back into the dash. With her left hand she put the pack of cigarettes back and put her hand on the top of the car door and with her right hand she turned on the radio and turned the dial slowly...which means her knee was still driving. Ron looked up and sighed. Yeah, her fucking knee was in charge of his fucking existence right now. It's a good thing there was traffic and they weren't able to go fast, right?

"Gunter glieben glauchen globen" the radio said as Stella settled on a station. Def Leppard was good for a drive to the hospital to watch a live birth, right? Sure, Ron might have preferred something like Ozzy Osbourne's "Crazy Train" to reflect his state of mind, but he was pretty sure this 1968 El Rustbucketo didn't have "Crazy Train." In fact, the radio was AM only, as was the state of mind in 1968 when it was built. Ron shuddered; how the fuck did people live in the time of AM radio only? The sonic deprivation would have killed him! Then again, he was dead anyway, so maybe living in the time of AM radio only wouldn't have been a problem.

The song ended just as Joe Elliot, the lead singer of Def Leppard, was replying to the age-old question "What do you want" with the age old answer "I want rock and roll, you betcha," in the same place the song always ends. No, wait, Ron thought, something's wrong. This song doesn't end that soon! It ends when Joe Elliott tells everybody that "we're gonna burn this damn place down, down to the ground." Ron wondered if anybody actually burned that damn place down, because obviously that damn place needed it, then quickly realized that a new song was starting. A country song. This station that Stella chose sure has a diverse playlist, he thought.

"Heeeeey, it's my truck, look at that...." Yeah, Ron thought, standard bro-country song about trucks. With somebody who sounded remarkably like Elvis Presley singing. Elvis singing country? That was a new one. Bro-country had really taken a weird turn, Ron thought.

"And, look at my head, girl, it's my big ass hat," Elvis-Soundalike sang, as Ron thought, yeah, standard bro-country about trucks and hats. With Elvis.

"And yeehaw, honey, it's an All-American zombie, driving a tractor through your fields and making it rain! All them zombies gotta get some brains!"

What.

The.

Fuck.

Ron considered this song. Bro-country music, sung by somebody who sounded like Elvis, about trucks, hats, tractors...and zombies? Weird. Sure, he understood that pop culture had embraced everything zombie, but bro-country music, Elvis, and zombies did not belong together. And besides, the song sucked, so he reached up and turned the AM radio tuning dial to the left.

"Zeeeeahhhhhhhhhbllllllllhhh.....woah, girl, them zombies like to party, when somebody smells it's a zombie farty...."

What.

The.

Fuck.

Again.

The same song? On a different station? Ron reached up and turned the dial to the left again until he found a different station.

"ACKLDLKEJOPIUDLKJSDLKJC.......when them zombies like to eat you know they start on the feet EVERYBODY GET YOUR GUNS AND LET'S MUNCH ON SOME HUMAN BUNS...."

Ron kept turning the dial to the left and to the right, like a pre-pubescent teenager searching for the Spice Channel on his cable system while his parents slept upstairs, and every single mother-fucking radio station was playing the zombie bro-country song.

Stella reached up with her right hand, her cigarette dangling from her mouth, her left hand on the steering wheel – FINALLY! – and turned it off. "What the fuck did you do to my radio, dad? What is that shit? Country Elvis zombie music on my rock and roll station? And my punk station? And my classical music station?"

She turned left off of the Vegas Strip towards VVVMMC, after sitting at a stoplight for three rounds and complaining 'who the fuck times these fucking lights?,' and gunned the El Camino until all of its 375 horses were purring. It was a beautiful cacophony of pre-catalytic converter American ingenuity and muscle.

"I didn't do it," Ron pleaded. "I don't know what the hell that was." Ron paused for a moment, thinking about what had just happened. It didn't make any sense, at all, and he had to say something. You know how sometimes unexpectedly strange events happen and everybody in the room or muscle car is completely baffled and you just have to ask about it? And if you don't ask about it your head is going to explode? It was exactly like that, except with zombies and daughters and Las Vegas.

"You like classical music?" There, Ron asked it. He felt a lot better asking the question, because really, he was baffled. His 17-year-old daughter was listening to classical music? She sure as shit didn't get that from him; Ron was, in his dead black heart, a rock and roll man, with an occasional foray into funk, R & B and heavy metal (on shitty days, when he needed the attitude). Classical music made as much sense to him as compassion made to a Republican politician.

Stella took a drag off of her cigarette as the El Camino headed west towards the hospital and exhaled the smoke into Ron's face. "Classical music calms me down, dad," she said with a glint in her eye that said, 'really, it calms me down. I'm not fucking kidding.' She reached down with her right hand while taking a drag with her left hand and steering the El Camino with her knee – Ron had given up trying to fight that – and turned the radio back on. *I don't give a damn about my reputation*, Joan Jett declared to the world through tinny 1968 mono speakers driven by a 1968 AM radio; the lack of sonic fidelity made it sound like she was making that declaration from former planet Pluto.

"Hey," Ron said, "The country zombie song is gone. Check the other channels."

"After Joan Jett, dad. This is my *jam*." Stella started singing Joan Jett's Bad Reputation at the top of her lungs, like she was trying to summon the ghost of Joan Jett back from the dead. It didn't matter that Joan Jett wasn't dead; Stella appeared to be trying to summon her. *I don't give a damn 'bout my reputation, You're living in the past it's a new generation, A girl can do what she wants to do and that's what I'm gonna do.*

Ron sighed, slumped down in his vinyl bucket seat, and let his zombie head fall to the right as the El Camino pulled up to a stoplight a mile from the hospital. Next to the car was a deep blue 1967 Pontiac Firebird with Cragar chrome wheels and raised white letter tires, like a 17 year-old had gotten a hold of the car to make it his chick magnet vehicle. And inside the car were zombies.

Ron sat up straight, rubbed his eyes, and looked at the adjacent lane and the Firebird again. What? Yep, zombies. The car was full of fucking zombies.

I don't give a damn 'bout my reputation, I've never been afraid of any deviation! And I don't really care if ya think I'm strange I ain't gonna change.... Stella was bouncing up and down in her own vinyl bucket seat and singing at the top of her lungs like a Muppet on speed while the El Camino idled at the stoplight...next to a Firebird full of zombies. Ron couldn't count how many; there was one driving, obviously, and one with a 'Zombie Lounge' shirt on, and there were passengers in the front and in the back and in the middle. The car had so many zombies in it that, from the outside, it looked like a tin of zombie sardines. Limbs and tendons and blood and duct tape inside the car everywhere...and every single zombie in the car was looking at Ron. And smiling.

Have you ever had a entire car full of zombies stare at you? Yeah, nobody in the entire history of time had...until this moment. Ron was a zombie himself, sure, but this was so straight up fucking weird that it froze his soul. Like a soul popsicle. Like getting brain freeze after eating an entire orange creamsicle bar in five seconds....but in your soul.

And I don't give a damn 'bout my reputation...The world's in trouble, there's no communication. And everyone can say what they want to say, it never gets better anyway. So why should I care 'bout a bad reputation anyway...Oh no, not me...Oh no, not me.

The light turned green ahead of the El Camino and the Firebird and every zombie in the Firebird laughed at Ron at the same exact time. The windows of both cars were closed and Stella and Joan Jett were singing along in the El Camino at a Spinal Tap-ish volume of 11, but Ron could still hear the zombie laughter coming from the Firebird.

Oh no, not me.

The laughter was the worst sound Ron had ever heard. It was the sound of 1,000 babies drowning. It was the sound of 47 kittens strung up by their tails. It was the sound of duct tape being ripped from somebody's testicles without regard for human capacity for pain.

Oh no, not me.

It was the sound of Ron's soul.

The world's in trouble, there's no communication.

It was the sound of the end of mankind. Again.

And then Ron realized he knew who was singing that bro-country song.

CHAPTER
8

Ron – Zombie.
Maria – Dilated seven cm.
Stella – Teenager.
Jim – Zombie and lovin' it!
Watson Son – In the birth canal.

Watching childbirth is one of the grossest and yet most beautiful things a human being can ever witness, outside of catching sight of your own huge brown log in the toilet bowl after eight consecutive days of painful constipation. Okay, watching childbirth is even more gross and yet more beautiful than that. It's like watching Miss America pick her nose. Okay, wait, watching childbirth is even more gross and beautiful than that, if that's possible. It's like sex on a public toilet. No, that's just gross. Nothing beautiful about that. Okay, then, watching childbirth is like... watching childbirth. Sometimes metaphors aren't necessary nor adequate.

As they pulled the El Camino into the parking lot of VVVMMC, Ron realized he hadn't watched childbirth in 17 years. And while the visage of a person coming out of another person, actually exiting another person, entering this world via its mother's exit passage, as it were, is so unique as to be branded on its viewer's cranium for some time, 17 years is a very long time. And Ron realized he couldn't remember much about it.

"The baby comes out of the earhole, right?" he jokingly asked Stella. And she hit him hard on his left arm.

"Ow! Fuck, honey, that's my only good arm!"

"You're so stupid, dad," she said, as she parked the El Camino in the handicapped parking spot by the hospital's entrance.

"I was joking. And you can't park here."

Stella looked at her dad like he was a fucking moron and pulled out a handicapped placard from underneath her seat. "I got this for you."

"I'm not handicapped."

"You're a zombie. And a fucking moron."

"Those are the only requirements to be handicapped now?"

"The baby comes out of the vagina, dad."

"The vajayjay?"

"The furburger."

"The meatpocket?"

"The wiener warmer."

"Fuckingham Palace?"

"The cum dumpster."

"Cum dumpster? That's fucking gross."

"And meatpocket isn't?" Stella grabbed her keys from the parked El Camino and hopped out of the car like a child in the parking lot of Disneyland. She threw her lit cigarette on the ground, stamped it out with her foot, and yelled at the top of her lungs, "Let's go get me a brother, bitch!"

Ron opened his door and got out of the car slowly and deliberately, more like a dad in the parking lot of Disneyland. "How do you know your brother's going to be a bitch? He's a boy! Wouldn't that make him more of a dick?"

"A prick?"

"A fuckface?"

"A douchebag?"

"You take it back, honey. Your brother is NOT going to be a douchebag. He can be a wiener warmer or a fuckface, but there's not way he's going to be a douchebag. NOT. IN. A. MILLION. YEARS." There was one type of person Ron couldn't stand, and that was, yes, the douchebag. Fucking jerk-ass overgrown frat boys with their spray tans and their steroid muscles and their sunglasses worn backwards on the back of their heads. Fuck those guys. If there were a douchebag buffet at one of the Vegas hotels, serving douchebags as zombie food, Ron would be first in line. And he'd stay all day.

"Wow, my zombie dad has standards." Ron could see the smirk on Stella's face as she stood in the hospital parking lot on the other side of the El Camino. Standards blahblahblah. As much as she was slamming him right now, he had to give her credit for her fantastic sarcasm. Ron had learned, through experience, that well-timed sarcasm could help any situation. If somebody was being a fuckface and you didn't want to explicitly point it out, sarcasm. If you wanted to make a douchebag's head spin on its orange neck, sarcasm. If you were surrounded by dumb people and wanted to figure out who was smart enough to understand sarcasm, sarcasm.

They approached the front door of the hospital and it automatically slid open. Just inside the door, Jim was talking to a police officer. Ron went over and gave Jim a big bear hug. A big zombie hug, really. Notably so because a piece of Ron's face stuck to the side of Jim's head when they hugged.

"Jim! I'm gonna be a daddy again!"

"Ron, they won't let me in."

"Can you believe it? After all these years, I'm gonna have another child! With Maria! And you're going to be the godfather! Let's go watch this boy come into this world through Fuckingham Palace!"

"I can't go in, Ron."

Ron started walking into the hospital and the police officer stopped him. "Can I see some ID, sir?"

Ron paused and looked at the police officer's badge. He was a captain. A captain, working a hospital entry? He looked at his name tag. 'Stubing.' "Uh, Captain Stubing, don't you recognize me?"

Captain Stubing lowered his douchebag sunglasses to the bridge of his nose and lifted his eyebrow as he looked Ron over. "Are you that one guy from that one thing?"

"EXACTLY. Thank you." Ron shook his head and started walking into the hospital as Captain Stubing's hand shot out and stopped him.

"That was sarcasm, sir. I don't recognize you."

Dammit, Ron thought, he was losing his touch. First of all, he missed the obvious sarcasm laid out in front of him like a douchebag buffet. Second of all, he was Ron Zombie, then he was Rob Zombie, and now he was nobody. Fuck. He reached into his pants and pulled out his newly acquired Nevada state ID. Maria had asked that he get it, as part of her attempts to make him into a shaped up family man, so he had gone down to the Nevada fucking DMV and fucking waited in fucking line for six fucking hours and finally procured it from a douchebag Nevada DMV clerk with, yes, orange skin. And Captain Douchelot of the SS Nevada fucking DMV had stamped across the ID, in big red letters, the word *ZOMBIE*. Ron showed it to Captain Stubing.

"You can't go in."

"But he's having a baby today and I'm going to be a big sister." Stella's face was red; clearly she was tired of waiting to share with her brother, at a nice young age, all the euphemisms for vagina.

From the halls of the hospital beyond came a sound. It started as a simple sigh, then evolved into a maniacal moan. Then it was like the hospital itself was in the middle of leaving its own huge brown log in the toilet bowl after eight consecutive days of painful constipation.

"WHHHHHHEEEEEEEEERRRRRRRRRREEEEEEEEEEEE EETTTTHHHHHHHEEEEEEEEEEEEFUUUUUUCKKKKKKK KKKKKARRRRRRRRREEEEEEEEEYOOOOOOOOU?"

Okay, so it was more of a question. A very loud question. So loud that when it was asked, everybody in the hospital covered their ears, as if everybody in the hospital were husbands being asked by their wives if they would please watch "Sex and the City 2" on Blu-Ray with them.

Ron recognized that loud question and that louder voice. Sure, he had only been dating Maria for a short while, but part of getting through the early parts of a relationship are making sure you understand and can deal with the other person's annoyed and annoying questions. No matter how annoyed and annoying they were. Hell, once you learn how to handle those, you can handle anything.

Ron motioned to Captain Stubing, who was now covering both of this ears with his hands with the motion that universally says *uncover at least one of your ears, I have something important to say*. Then, when Stubing had one ear partially uncovered, Ron yelled as loud as he could "THAT'S MY FIANCEE" just as Maria stopped screaming.

The earth froze on its axis and the lobby of the hospital went silent. Every single person in it turned and glared at Ron like he had just announced he had given everybody SARS. No, he realized, it was more like an Ebola stare.

Captain Stubing uncovered both of his ears. "Why didn't you say so? She's been calling for you for some time."

"At that volume?"

"Yes, at that volume."

"Sorry, man." Ron felt an instant kinship with the captain; if two men can't bond over annoying questions from women, what can they bond over? Ron realized this made him a douchebag and apologized to himself. Then he congratulated himself internally for knowing where the douchebag line was. It would help him raise his son to not go over that line.

"Dad, let's go!" Stella clearly wasn't interested in Ron's internal douchebag dialogue.

"Can I go?" Ron asked the captain.

Everybody in the lobby, still glaring at Ron like they had just found out he had given them Ebola, replied at the same time. "GO!" It was like being told by a whole neighborhood of irritated moms that it was time to go the fuck to school so they could have their morning wine.

Ron, Stella and Jim started quickly walking towards the inner workings of the hospital, towards the constipated sound. Captain Stubing reached out and grabbed Jim by his arm. "Not you."

"But I'm the kid's, uh, uncle!" Jim lied.

"You're a fucking zombie."

"So is he!" Jim was pointing at Ron.

Captain Stubing wasn't letting go of Jim's arm, and some of the skin was coming off in his grip. "The Zombie Rights Act, passed last week, says that zombies aren't allowed in hospitals unless they're directly related to somebody having a baby."

"What the fuck?" Jim asked.

"The Zombie Rights Act. You've never heard of it?"

"No."

Ron and Stella stood just inside the lobby, watching Jim. This was stupid, Ron thought. We're all human beings here. Or we used to be.

"The Republicans passed it last week in response to all the zombies walking around. You can't go in hospitals 'cuz they're afraid you'll think you're in a buffet or a smorgasbord, so you gotta stay outside. 'Cuz you know, there aren't people outside." Captain Stubing chuckled at his own sarcasm and rolled his eyes, as if to say, *This is stupid. We're all human beings here, except for you fucking zombies.*

"WHHHHHHEEEEEEEEERRRRRRRRRREEEEEEEEEEEE EETTTTHHHHHHHEEEEEEEEEEEFUUUUUUCKKKKKKKK KKKKKARRRRRRRRREEEEEEEEEYOOOOOOOOU?"

"Dad, let's go, she's about to have the baby!" Stella grabbed Ron's arm, pulling a bit of skin off in the process. His newly exposed blood smelled delicious, Ron thought. Fuck.

"Is that what having a baby sounds like? I think I blocked that out of my memory." Ron also began working on blocking the smell of his own blood out of his memory, 'cuz that was gross. He could handle being a zombie, but he never wanted to get to the point where he was eating himself. What would that be called? Auto-zombieism?

"Yes, dad, that's what it fucking sounds like! Let's go! Jim, do you want the keys to my car?"

"No, thanks," Jim replied. "I'll hang around outside in case you need anything. Maybe I'll find someone to eat on the poop deck." Captain Stubing lifted his left eyebrow and, with his eyes, threw a look at Jim that said, *You're not a fucking human being but you better eat like one so I don't have to shoot you in the fucking head. And don't make a 'Love Boat' joke again or I'll shoot you in the fucking head.* Jim saw the look and raised his hand. "I was kidding. KIDDING! I'll get some*thing* to eat. I'm actually a vegetarian zombie. Should I ask Julie McCoy where to look?" Ron and Jim both giggled like little girls who had just placed a Whoopee Cushion on their teacher's chair. Vegetarian zombie, Ron thought, that's a good one. I might need to use that one.

Jim went back towards the hospital entrance to the sliding glass doors. "Good luck in there! BRAINS!" Captain Stubing glared at him again. "KIDDING! Jeez! Sensitive much?"

Once Jim was out the front door, Ron and Stella took off running towards the sound of Maria loudly wondering where the fuck they were. Ron hoped he would be a good enough boyfriend to her that he wouldn't ever have to hear that sound again, but he also knew that right now it was completely warranted. She was probably in labor – do zombies still have labor? – and in a lot of pain – do zombies still have pain? – but, Ron surmised, she was probably in good hands. VVVMC was a modern facility, based on its lobby, and he suspected his girlfriend was being taken care of in a luxurious hospital maternity suite, with the best drugs, administered by a female doctor who knew exactly what the fuck she was doing.

Of course, none of that was true. When he and Stella followed the sound of Ron's girlfriend anticipating his son coming out of her zombie vagina – now THERE'S a sentence, Ron thought – he ended up at a closet.

A closet.

How did he know? It said "closet" on the door.

What.

The.

Fuck.

Ron opened the closet door and, yep, sure enough, behind the door was his girlfriend, lying on a folding table, surrounded by walls of electrical boxes and janitorial supplies, being attended to by a male doctor. Stella pushed Ron out of the way and burst into the closet. "SERIOUSLY? My brother's being born in a fucking closet?"

The doctor turned around; she looked at Stella. Yep, Ron thought, he was a she, not a he. It must have been the short hair.

"We're only allowed to deliver zombie babies in closets here," the doctor said. "Part of the Zombie Protection Act. I'm not even sure how you zombies are getting pregnant, zombie sex sounds gross, but obviously you are and here we are."

"I'm not a fucking zombie," Stella said, "and they're probably zombie fucking. Have you considered that?"

Ron looked at the doctor's name tag; Doctor Roberts. Okay. "Listen, Doctor Roberts, first of all, zombie sex isn't bad – as long as you don't think about eyeballs – and second of all -"

The doctor turned in the tiny hospital closet, nearly elbowing Stella in the boob, saw Ron...and her face lit up. "You're Ron Zombie."

"Yes, I am," Ron said. "And she's -"

"She's YOUR wife?"

"Girlfriend."

"Well, shit, why didn't you say so?" The doctor started unbuttoning her white doctor coat. Oh, shit, Ron said, what was she doing? Was she undressing? Did she want to have my zombie baby, too? Maybe I shouldn't have extolled the virtues of zombie sex so vigorously! Couldn't she see I was taken? Could he stand another woman yelling at the top of her lungs for him from a maternity ward closet? That might be a lot for one day.

Ron closed his eyes as Doctor Roberts flung open her smock, revealing a 'Ron Zombie Brains' t-shirt beneath it that Ron couldn't see because his eyes were closed. Duh.

"I'm a big fan, Ron."

Ron opened one eye slowly, hoping Doctor Roberts wasn't standing there in front of him, his daughter, and his pregnant girlfriend with no clothes on. That might have been the most awkward moment of the day, and that was saying a lot considering they were about to watch his girlfriend give birth. Birth was usually the most awkward moment of whatever day on which it occurred, to the people involved in the event.

"Let's get you and your girlfriend into the celebrity wing of the hospital."

Ron opened both eyes quickly and saw Doctor Roberts pointing to her Ron Zombie shirt. Um, okay?

"The what?"

"The celebrity ward. You're a celebrity, and we have a special ward for you."

Um, okay? "Um, okay. That would be great."

"Can I get your autograph on my shirt?"

"First?" Stella was standing there, in all her punk rock attitude, not being very punk rock at all. What's more punk rock than getting your shirt autographed before you deliver a zombie baby?

"No, you're right, young lady. We can do it later. Can I take a selfie with you and your new zombie baby, Ron?"

"AFTER," Stella replied as she pushed the doctor out the closet door. "Get us to the celebrity wing first, doctor."

"WHERETHEFUCKAREYOOOOOOU?" Maria cried out as her maternity bed traveled through the hospital hallway. Ron leaned over and gave her a kiss on the lips; she was beautiful, the most beautiful zombie he had ever seen, even as she seemed ready to eat his brains. But Ron remembered this part of giving birth; his ex-wife Erika was like this with Stella. Ron suggested to himself that men should really wear protective gear when they went to a birth so they don't get hurt. That might help men relate to it, he realized. It was kinda like a sporting event, right?

Doctor Roberts, who was watching Ron the whole time they were walking and looking at him like she was twelve years old and it was 1976 and he was Shaun Cassidy, stopped them at a gold plated door. "Ron, welcome to the celebrity ward."

She swiped the card around her neck on the door and it opened; to Ron it was like using his golden ticket to get into Willy Wonka's Chocolate Factory. Coming from the drab simple white of the main hospital corridor and rooms, they entered a utopia of unseen proportions. Hawaii, basically. With Bell Biv Devoe, the 1990s hip-hop/funk/soul/pop group.

"You ready, Ron?" One of the Bell Biv Devoe group pointed at Ron and spoke. Ron didn't which one it was; Bell? Biv? Devoe? Did it fucking matter?

"You talking to me?" Ron asked.

"Spiderman and Freeze in full effect." Biv was speaking now. Or maybe it was Bell. Ron really didn't fucking know.

"Girl, I must warn you...." Oh, Ron thought, they're playing their song "Poison." That's what was going on.

Ron looked around at the celebrity ward as seven nurses appeared and took Maria's maternity bed and wheeled it along a corridor of plush ocean-colored carpet. Ron and Stella followed along as the drab white walls of the non-celebrity ward were replaced with the plantation-like shutters and miniature palm trees of the celebrity ward. A butler appeared – or at least he looked like a butler, Ron thought, with his black tuxedo and bow tie, white butler-y shirt, and silver platter. With beer on it.

BEER.

Ron giggled. Stella smirked. The butler bowed.

It was all like Ron's best dream come true, and he participated by taking a beer – an IPA, based on the color and smell of the beer in the glass – and thanking the butler.

"Situation is serious..." Devoe was singing the next line of the song. Or maybe it was Biv. It didn't matter, Ron thought, because BEER.

Ron took a sip of his beer as they walked along the Hawaiian beach that had somehow made its way into Vegas Valley View Medical Center. He then realized Stella also had a beer. He sighed; she was too young legally, but he knew she was as nervous about this as he was and she was mature emotionally. As long as she wasn't driving them home anytime soon, right?

The butler spoke. "Don't worry about her drinking, sir. We'll have a limousine waiting after the birth to take you all home. Oh, and young lady, your car is being detailed. 1968 El Camino, yes?"

Stella giggled. "Yes."

"We'll have it dropped off at your apartment. After we paint it. Same color?"

Stella's eyes grew wide, like she'd just seen a zombie. "Uh, yeah, sure!? No, wait, paint it black. Matte black."

"Okay. We have some nice 5-spoke Cragar rims for it, with some raised white letter tires. May we install those as well?"

"Uh, okay!" Stella looked at Ron sideways as they walked through the Hawaiian corridor. He shrugged his shoulders, because what the fuck?

Doctor Roberts turned the maternity bed into a room with a bamboo ceiling, wicker furniture, a bamboo floor, and a giant electric palm frond fan overhead. Ron looked around and turned to the butler.

"Is your whole hospital like this?" he asked.

"No sir, only the celebrity ward."

"That's fucked up," Stella said, "and so fucking awesome!" She threw herself on a pappasan chair in the corner of the room and disappeared in the oversized and overstuffed cushion, reminding Ron of those times when Stella was young and would make blanket forts all over their apartment.

"WHHHHHEEEEEEEEEEEEEEEEEEEEEE." Clearly Maria wasn't in the mood for nostalgia, but she sounded like she was actually having…fun?

"Did you give her the epidural already?" Ron asked Doctor Roberts.

"No, but she's dilated enough for one. Seven centimeters."

"Is that a lot?"

"It's almost enough to have a baby. Sign my shirt? I brought a Sharpie."

Doctor Roberts handed Ron a pen and he signed her shirt. "RON….ZOMBIE. BRAINS." Doctor Roberts smiled as the butler reappeared with more beer, which Ron gladly took. Sure, he hated being a celebrity, but not right now. Right now, being a celebrity was the difference between being in Hawaii and being in antiseptic hell. And everybody would choose Hawaii over antiseptic hell, right?

Ron looked at the window of the room and saw painted palm trees, a painted ocean, and Jim. And zombies. Lots and lots of zombies. Swaying zombies, singing a song that Ron knew. *Whoa, girl, them zombies like to party,when somebody smells it's a zombie farty.* It was like being at a college fraternity after the keg had run out. He waved at Jim and mouthed the words *be careful*, as Jim waved back before he was pushed out of the picture by zombies. Lots and lots of zombies. Ron shivered, and then was reminded he had more important things to worry about right now.

"BAAAAAAAAAABY." Yeah, that.

"You ready, Ron?" Doctor Roberts had buttoned up her coat and was tending to Maria's vagina.

Her Fuckingham Palace.

Ron chuckled at his own joke. Reincorporation always made him laugh.

"Dad, fucking get ready!" Stella was standing over by Maria now, too. "Are you thinking about her vagina again, Dad?" She rolled her eyes. "Jeez!"

"NO!" Damn, Ron, realized, his daughter knew him very well. He looked over at the zombie window; that wasn't important now, 'cuz he had a birth to take care of first. "Okay, doc, what do I need to do?"

"You're in the celebrity ward, Mister Zombie, you don't have to do anything. Sit back, relax, drink a beer, and let our team of professionals handle everything."

"WHHHHEEEEEEEEEERRRRRRRRRRRREEEEEEEEE-AAAAAAAAAAARRRRRRRRRREEEEEEEEEYOU?"

"Um, I should probably participate."

"Dad!"

"No, actually, I WANT to participate. This is my zombie baby. Actually, it's a human baby, but both of its parents are zombies, so I keep calling it -"

"That girl is poi-son!" Bell Biv Devoe were in the maternity room, singing and dancing like it was MTV in 1991 or some shit. Yeah, Ron realized, the fact that he could place the song in a certain year bothered him, too.

"Okay, Mister Zombie, you can participate. Most celebrity spouses don't even show up for the births, but once in awhile somebody wants to be involved…"

"YOOOOOOOOOOU!" Maria obviously wanted him to participate, but more importantly Ron wanted to be involved with this. He never thought he'd get a second chance to be a parent, and he regretted, on many levels, the shitty parent and spouse he was the first time around, so, given a second chance, he was going to do it right. Which means he was going to be involved with the birth, no matter how gross it might be. And it would be gross, no doubt about that, but Maria was the love of his life, so…

"BRAINS!" Ah, Ron thought, there she was, the love of his life. If she was spouting out their favorite word, everything was going to be alright.

"Brains, honey," he replied.

From outside the window, Ron could hear the gathered zombies. "BRRRRAAAAAAAIIIIIIIIIINSSSSS!" The glass in the window shook and he glanced over; there were security bars across the window on the outside, and he took a deep breath. He wasn't sure that the zombies' version of "BRAINS" was the same as he and Maria's version, which was more like two humans calling each other mushy names like 'sweetums' and shit like that. And, frankly, he didn't want to find out. Wars have started over lesser disagreements. And if the window was shaking, there were a lot of zombies out there. Ron hoped Jim was okay but he also knew that if anybody could handle themselves in a horde of zombies, Jim could. It would be a lot like hanging out with a bunch of hungover tourists on the Vegas Strip, and Jim was very good at that. He would just start cracking zombie jokes and make a shitload of friends.

And then the zombies started singing again. Muffled through the window, but Ron still knew the song. *Heeeeey, it's my truck, look at that. And, look at my head, girl, it's my big ass hat. And yee-haw, honey, it's an All-American zombie...*

"Mister Zombie – can I call you Ron?"

"What?"

"Ron, she's almost ready." Doctor Roberts stepped aside.

"That's. Right. Ron, it's time. For the birth. Of your zombie/human baby." Ron recognized that voice; it was Howard Cosell, longtime play-by-play announcer for Monday Night Football, as well as boxing, the Olympics, and, ahem, *Battle of the Network Stars.* Howard Cosell's voice was ingrained into Ron's head, just like it was ingrained into the head of every man who grew up in that era. "Hi everybody, and welcome to Monday Night Birthball."

Two things, Ron thought: Birthball? And didn't Howard Cosell die in 1995?

A shambling zombie shambled into Ron's view and yep, it was Howard Cosell. Ron knew because he was wearing a yellow blazer, a white dress shirt, and a dark brown tie; all things Cosell wore when he was on TV announcing the Olympics, boxing, MNF, or, ahem, *Battle of the Network Stars.* The zombie's face looked a lot like what you'd think a Cosell zombie's face would look like: Like Howard Cosell had been dead for 20 years and had somehow hung around on this earth, above ground. George Clooney he was not.

"The pregnant lady has taken her spot on the bed; grab a drink everybody and sit back and enjoy this play-by-play of this live birth, brought. To. You. By. Zombieade," Zombie Cosell said, in his trademark stop/start/stop/start style, which did not sound unlike Christopher Walken as your dad, lecturing you on the virtues of going to college.

"Zombieade!" Bell Biv Devoe must have been sponsored by Zombieade as well, because they had just changed the chorus of their song "Poison." Ron chuckled. This whole thing was so fucking weird – Bell Biv Devoe, Zombie Howard Cosell, the Celebrity Ward at the Vegas Valley View Memorial Hospital, and Maria about to give birth to something – that he decided to do what Cosell said, so he swigged a drink from his beer and prepared to enjoy the play-by-play. Of whatever was about to happen.

"And. We're. Off, ladies and gentlemen," Zombie Cosell said, as Biv – or maybe it was Devoe – handed him what looked like a turkey leg and he took a bite and swallowed. "This birth – not the play-by-play, just the birth – brought to you by Human Farms, where they grow the Best. Damn. Zombie. Food. You. Could. Ever. Want."

Human Farms, Ron thought. What the fuck?

Zombie Cosell wiped some blood from his chin on his yellow blazer and looked at Ron. "You sure you're ready for this, young zombie? You look pale."

"Isn't that a natural fucking look for a zombie?"

"WHHHERRRRRREEEEEEETHHHHHEEEEEEEE-FFFFFFFFFFUUUUUUUUUCCCCCKKKKKARRREEYOU?"

"AND. WE. HAVE. HEAD!" Zombie Cosell exclaimed as he looked toward a screaming Maria.

Ron heard the word "head" and did what any normal American male would do when hearing the word 'head': he leaped up and spilled his IPA down the front of his shirt. He looked around and quickly realized that the 'head' in question was not the 'head' he had in mind. No, instead, emerging from his girlfriend's Fuckingham Palace was a tiny little sphere, not unlike a grapefruit. Doctor Roberts stopped glaring at Ron like he was all five members of the Osmond Brothers in 1974 and turned to Maria. "Holy shit, that was fast. Honey, do you need an epidural?"

"GEEEEEETTTTTTTTTTTTTIIIIIIIIIIIIIIIIIII-TTTTTTTTTTTTTTTOOOOOOOOOOUUUUUUUTTTT!" Maria exclaimed. It was more than an exclamation, really, it was more of a command. A demand. A 'do this before I rip your fucking head off' kind of thing.

At that moment, the room filled with a sound that reminded Ron of his days working in food service; it was the sound of a particularly pressurized magnum of champagne being opened for a party: "POP!"

Ron looked over and his girlfriend's vagina was as open as a DMV at noon on a Tuesday, which is to say it was very, very open. And sticking out of it? A tiny child, who looked exactly like a mini version of Ron, covered in something that looked like a combination of pizza sauce, cream of mushroom soup, and kibble.

"He could go all. The. Way!" Zombie Howard Cosell was very enthusiastic about this birth, obviously. The child sticking out of Maria's Fuckingham Palace shot into the doctor's arms, like it couldn't wait to get into the world and see what was it all about, and Ron could see it had a penis. And balls. Swollen balls. Ron had a son! And his son had big balls! The moment washed over Ron like a tsunami over an unsuspecting Pacific Rim country and Ron passed out…as most men do when presented with something so artistic and beautiful. On his way to the floor, Ron heard Howard Cosell yell, "Down! Goes! Zombie! Down! Goes! Zombie!"

Ron woke to the smell of salt; he hoped it was on a femur that had been delicately prepared to his liking – that is to say that it was bloody and fresh – but he didn't have that kind of luck. No, the salt was a smelling salt, and it was being waved under his nose by Doctor Robert.

"We lost you for a minute there, Mister Zombie."

Ron shook his head and realized his mental cobwebs were no match for the smelling salts, which was probably good. He was awake. He looked around the room; Maria was on the bed, the mushroom/pizza sauce/kibble placenta was in a bowl on the bed, and the zombies were still at the window, singing that horrible country song. Oh, and Zombie Howard Cosell was interviewing Ron.

"So, Ron, great birth today. Are you proud of the way your guys hung in there and pulled this one out at the end?"

"What?"

"You knew this would be no cakewalk, and it wasn't pretty, but you'll take it, right?"

What the fuck was Zombie Howard Cosell talking about?

"It was a total team effort, right? This birth was for the fans, right?" Zombie Howard Cosell gestured towards the window where Jim and all the zombies were singing and clamoring to get in.

Oh, Ron thought, I get it. Fucking Zombie Howard Cosell was speaking only in sports metaphors. He decided to play along, because how often to get to be interviewed by Howard Cosell? Zombie, human, or otherwise?

"Oh, hell yes, Howard, a birth is a birth, and this was a good birth for us," Ron said, leaning down into the microphone like he was in a locker room "This was a confidence booster; we knew what we had to do and we went out and did it." Ron smiled at Stella, who had a camera out and was taking a picture of the surreal scene.

"Everyone counted you out before the birth started," Stella said, as she giggled and took pictures of Ron and Zombie Howard Cosell.

"That's right, honey," Ron said, winking at Stella. "It feels great; you dream about this moment as a kid, from the moment you start noticing members of the opposite sex, you know? But we still have work to do; we're going to use this birth as a stepping stone to the next level."

"Well, Ron, you shocked. The. World," Zombie Howard Cosell said, in his signature style. "Congratulations. Now, Ron, we have one more topic to deal with before we leave."

Oh, shit, Ron thought, this was all coming to an end. Cops were gonna show up because of the Zombie Right Act or whatever and they were gonna take Ron and Maria and their human baby away to live on some reservation out in Spokane or South Dakota or some shit for the rest of their lives and the next generation's lives and so on and so on and who would want that? Nobody! He assumed a kung-fu stance and started towards Howard Cosell. He figured Cosell was the most famous person in the room and if the coppers were going to try to send him to a reservation he was going to take Cosell hostage first and negotiate his way out of it. 'Negotiate.' Ron giggled at his own ambition.

"What. Are. You going to name the boy?" Cosell asked.

Ron stopped his kung-fu stance just as he was about to karate chop Zombie Cosell about his face and shoulders. Name? The boy?

"Yes, Ron, what are we going to name the boy?" Maria chimed in from the bed.

"Sue," Stella said, from the Eames chair, where she was drinking a beer. "Johnny Cash would like it."

"Jasper?" Doctor Roberts said, without looking up from whatever she was doing to Maria's vagina. "We've never had a Jasper."

"Humperdink?" Stella said. "Fenton? Justin Bieber?" She and Doctor Roberts both laughed at that one.

"That boy is Robiiiiiin," Bell Biv Devoe sang.

"Douchebag Dave." Stella was obviously not taking this seriously, and Ron glared at her. She knew how he felt about douchebags!

"Lancelot?" Doctor Roberts said, without looking up from whatever she was doing to Maria's placenta. "We've never had a Lancelot."

"STOP," Ron said. "Those are all, ahem, good suggestions, I guess, but his name will be Ron Junior. Right honey?"

"Right," Maria said, without looking up from watching the doctor do something to the placenta. Ron had heard that some people eat it afterwards, and he realized that he and Maria had never discussed this particular part of their relationship, but that he hoped she wasn't going to to eat it. Sure, it might have been nutritious, but gross! In that way, placenta is like kale.

And then Ron wondered what other parts of their relationship they hadn't discussed that they probably should have before they agreed to have a relationship and to bring a child into this crazy zombie world. Things like:

- Do you eat with your mouth open or closed?
- Do you talk with food in your mouth?
- When you snore, is it a Prius or a Mack Truck?
- Is dirty underwear stuck to the wall considered art or laundry gone bad?

Howard Cosell spoke. "Human life is sports in microcosm, ladies and gentlemen. This. Is. Howard. Cosell…..signing off. Stay tuned for a word from our sponsor.."

The lights in the room dimmed and Bel Biv Devoe started singing the jingle from "Human Farms":

Human farms,
Don't have to beg,
Come for the arms,
Stay for the legs…

A nurse put Ron Junior into Ron's arms and Stella smiled at Ron. He smiled back, looked at his son in his arms, and realized all of a sudden that he had never felt more human.

Doctor Roberts came over, sat next to Ron on the bed, pulled out her phone, and took a selfie with both Junior and Ron, who realized all of a sudden that he had never felt less human.

CHAPTER
9

Ron – Zombie.
Maria – Mombie.
Stella – Big Sister!
Jim – Zombie, and lovin' it!
Ron Junior – Poopin' diapers, yo!

When a couple decides to have a child or, as is often the case, finds the decision to have a child made for them by A) a wild night of alcohol-fueled passion, B) a wild night of drug-fueled passion, or C) a morning quickie brought on by zombie lust and a beautiful woman in a hockey jersey, there are millions and billions of other decisions for the new parents to make. Decisions such as the child's name, cloth diapers versus disposable diapers, stroller versus roller skates...okay, maybe not that one...and how the fuck are we going to pay for this child and all of the associated expenses?

"I want to be a stay-at-home mom," Maria whispered in Ron's ear one morning whilst breast-feeding Ron Junior in their bed. She was wearing a frilly red thing – that was Ron's technical term for it – and it showcased her currently overly-ample zombie-bosom. Ron loved her zombie-bosom, always, but not right now; once the object of your affection becomes a food truck, some of the grandeur of the object dissipates, like rain on a sunny day. And Junior was this food truck's best customer; nay, he was its only customer. Ron pined for the day the food truck was returned to him in its former condition: all truck, no food.

"Don't you mean a stay-at-home zombie?" Ron asked as he let his fingers lollygag on her bare arm. "My ZILF?"

"ZILF?" Maria asked, her face alight with a smile. "BRAINS!"

"BRAINS!" Ron screeched in return, his face alight in agreement.

"WAAAAAAH" Ron Junior cried, his face alight in bewilderment. 'BRAINS' was an inside joke between the two zombies in the room and the human obviously didn't find it very funny.

"Sorry Junior," Ron whispered to Ron Junior as he stroked his baby's head, which at this young age was closer to a cantaloupe that somebody had dropped in the grocery store than anything else. It was the most adorable cantaloupe Ron had ever seen or touched, and he worked in a grocery store in high school, so that was a high compliment indeed.

"Stay-at-home zombie, sure, whatever." Maria's sapphire blue eyes perforated Ron's head like a three-hole punch; she was a sublime creature, zombie or human. Ron would do anything for her at this moment. "I think you should go get a job."

Okay, maybe not that, Ron thought. A job? What. The. Fuck?

"A job?"

"Yes, honey, a job. Ron Junior's going to need more diapers and formula and a jogging stroller and and and AND…"

Holy fuck, Ron thought, a baby needs a lot of shit. Because a baby does a lot of shit. And his baby right now smelled like shit.

"Goddamn, he's stinky."

"He shit, honey."

"Obviously."

"Will you change him?"

"What if I don't want him to change? I like him just as he is." Ron looked at Ron Junior, with his flesh-crayon-colored skin and his cantaloupe head and his chubby arms and the little bit of umbilical cord still attached to his bellybutton and thought, yeah, he's perfect. No changing necessary.

"No, doofus, change his diaper."

"Wait, me?"

"Um, yes, you're his daddy."

Ron looked around the room of Maria's apartment – which, really, was both Ron and Maria's apartment now – the mini-blinds keeping the Vegas November afternoon sun from igniting the room, the 16 muscle cars parked outside, the hot, gorgeous, nearly naked blonde zombie holding their baby next to him on the double bed with the 40-count cotton sheets and wondered, how the fuck did I get here?

"Surely you've changed a diaper before?"

Yes, he had, but he was human then. And he had use of both of his arms. And he was human. AND HE HAD USE OF BOTH OF HIS ARMS. He thought maybe, just maybe, he was at a bit of a disadvantage this time. Then again, if the drummer for Def Leppard can play "Rock of Ages" with only one arm, night after night, for 20,000 screaming fans, Ron could change a diaper, with only one arm, for one screaming fan.

"Yes, of course I have."

"The diapers are right over there." Maria pointed to a bag of Huggies across the room on the dresser.

"WAAAAH" Ron Junior exclaimed, which Ron took to mean, 'Hurry up, bitch! This rash on my asshole isn't getting any less asshole rash-ier!' Children these days. Such brats. Ron thought he should teach his kid some respect…when his kid was old enough to understand what respect was.

"I got 'em." Ron rolled off the bed and walked over to the dresser; good thing he still had use of both of his legs. He reached down with his left arm and grabbed the Huggies; good thing they had a handle. Back when he was human he would have mocked whoever the fuck had the idea to put a handle on diapers, but now that he was arm-capacity-limited he got it. In his one-armed zombie state he 'got' a lot things that didn't make any sense when he was human. It was a lot like understanding most rock n' roll songs after a woman dumps you.

He brought one Huggie – is that the right term for a single diaper? – back to the bed and set it next to Ron and laid back down. And did nothing else.

"WAAAAAAAH" Ron Junior said, with conviction.

"He wants YOU to change him," Ron said to Maria. "He just said so."

"Bullfuckingshit. You need to know how to do this."

"Why?"

Maria's face sagged like a building collapsing and Ron realized at this moment that this was the wrong question to ask a recently pregnant woman...zombie...thing. Either way, he realized he was being a jackass. "Sorry, you're right."

Ron picked up the Huggie with his working hand, shook it like a Polaroid Picture, chuckled, and laid it down on the bed, supine, ready for child. It felt a bit like preparing a peanut butter and jelly sandwich; the diaper was the bread and Junior was the peanut butter. Actually, more like it, Ron realized he was preparing a burrito, one of his favorite meals when he was human. Carne Asada, Chicken, Pork...he loved all burritos equally. He was an equal opportunity burritist.

"HONEY! Are you thinking about burritos again?" Damn, Ron thought, we've only been together a short time and she already knows me that well! Maybe our zombie brains have melded or something.

"Yes. Sorry."

"WAAAAAAAAAAAH!"

"Will you please change his diaper? I have to go to the bathroom." Maria got up from the bed, her frilly red thing hanging up on her back just long enough for Ron to admire her bare zombie-ass sashaying to the bathroom like it owned the place. Maria's zombie-ass, post-childbirth, post zombie-turn, still did own the place, really. It looked like two halves of a fresh avocado that had just been split open. Except it was flesh colored, not green. Yet. Ron wondered if she would decay enough to turn green and then threw up in his mouth a little bit.

"Okay, Junior, here we go. Just like a burrito."

Ron Junior looked up at Ron and wailed. "WAAAAAAAAA-AAAAAAAAAAH." Fuck, Ron thought, maybe he knows I'm a zombie. Maybe he knows I'm dead and I'm really not qualified to be his father. Or the paterfamilias of this family…or whatever the fuck it was. Paterzombilias? Ron realized he could publish a zombie dictionary of words he had made up that related to his predicament and probably sell a few. To zombies. Who read. Ha! Do zombies read? Ron did, but what about other zombies? Were there other zombies? Of course there were, Ron realized, because he had seen them. But how many? And where? Who? What? When? Where? Wh – "WAAAAAAAAAH"

Fuck, Ron remembered, I'm a father. Time to focus. "Okay, Junior, would you like white rice or brown rice? Black beans or pinto? What kind of meat?" Ron Junior looked up at his father and made one of those cute little baby faces that said, *You are fucking crazy, I'm not really a burrito. CHANGE MY DIAPER OR I'M GOING TO CRY AND THEN MY HOT ZOMBIE MOM IN THE HOCKEY JERSEY WILL NEVER FUCK YOU AGAIN. EVER.*

Ron heard Maria flush the toilet in the bathroom, saw the space behind Ron Junior's face load up with tears as if he was preparing to let loose a Colorado River of waaaaaaaaaaaah, and realized his son was right. If he ever wanted to get laid again, he better attend to his fatherly duties.

Ron rolled Junior over with his left hand onto the diaper, so that he was face down on the bed, and the diaper was in the right place, right over his tiny little penis. Still, Ron remembered something about not letting a baby be face down on a bed for very long, because they die when they can't breathe, duh, so he grabbed Junior with one hand and flipped him back over onto his back. With the diaper next to him on the bed. Of course.

Ron looked at this situation, with his newborn baby on the bed and the diaper, which wanted to be on the newborn baby, next to the newborn baby on the bed, and he thought of high school math class. *If a newborn baby train going 50 miles an hour leaves Charleston at 10:30am heading west and a diaper train going 45 miles an hour leaves San Francisco at 110 miles an hour heading east, where the fuck do they meat?* Meat! Fuck, Ron was hungry. And he still had fatherly duties to attend to. Here's a baby, here's a diaper, here's a zombie with one good arm, how does the diaper get on the baby? It was like a Rubik's Cube for the Damned.

Ron lifted up Junior's legs to prepare to drag him over to the diaper, and Junior projectile shat all over Joaquin's 'Girls Direct To You' shirt that Ron was wearing. Maria came out of the bathroom, resplendent in her frilly red thing and her freshly made up face, and looked at Ron, who was covered in baby shit and not nearly as resplendent.

"You need help, honey?"

Ron Watson, who had never really felt like he needed help ever, knew that this time he was up against a formidable foe, the likes of which he had never, ever seen, nor imagined: zombie parenthood. Zombie parenthood is a task not for the faint of heart, nor for a lone, single-armed zombie. He swallowed his pride – it went down like an eyeball, in that he knew it was going to come up again later, at the most inconvenient time possible – and turned to face the love of his zombie life, his partner, his teammate in raising little Ron Junior, and simply said, "Yes."

And while the love of his zombie life, his partner, his teammate began changing the diaper that he himself could not change, she suggested again that she thought he should get a job.

Ron pondered this for a second. He didn't need a job, he could just figure out where the drug dealers and pimps in Vegas lived and go eat them and take their money, right?

Maria looked over from changing Ron's diaper; Ron noticed she wasn't covered in baby shit like he was. The mother/son relationship had perks that the father/son relationship obviously lacked. "You're not thinking about eating drug dealers again, are you honey?"

Fuck, Ron thought, yes, I fucking am. Damn, she knows me well.

"Um, noooooo, I'm thinking about -"

"You have that look in your eye."

"What look?"

"That look. That cute *I'm lying and everybody can see it* look. It's cute…but you're lying. And everybody can see it, even Junior." Ron Junior giggled.

Ron knew he couldn't lie to either of them, ultimately, but especially to her. There are lies that all fathers tell their sons, to help them get through life, lies like, *If you make that face it's going to stay like that forever*, and, *that Halloween candy isn't good for you, so give it to me*, but he couldn't lie to Maria. He liked her too much; nay, he loved her too much, to take the relationship in that direction. This relationship, this family, had to be built on trust. It was one of the few things he was sure of right now. So he spoke the truth.

"I was thinking about eating drug dealers *and* pimps, actually."

Maria held Ron Junior up with her arms under his armpits; he was fully dressed in his baby KISS onesie that the doctor had given him. How the fuck, Ron wondered, did she get him dressed so fast? In a onesie?

"I know you were." Maria raised her eyebrows as if to say, "And?"

"And what?"

"And you're not going to, right?"

"But honey, it's so easy! I get to eat, I get paid, and I'm doing a public service by cleaning up the streets!"

Maria looked at Ron, her face a stone cold lion. The earth froze on its axis again and the room grew as heavy as a skyscraper atop a skyscraper atop a third skyscraper. Finally, she spoke, the urgency in her voice as palpable as the taste of mold on moldy bread. "I know it sounds easy, Ronald James Watson, but being a zombie is dangerous, and you're only making it more dangerous by acting like a fucking zombie! I lost my husband, I will NOT lose another soul mate to fucking zombie...zombie...zombieism...whatever the fuck it's called!" If she were human, she would have been crying; instead, she dry-sobbed for several moments, which made Ron Junior cry, his tears dripping onto his KISS onesie, which made it look like Gene Simmons was crying as well. Ron put his left arm around Maria and flung his right arm around Gene, creating the weirdest group hug ever, and spoke the truth.

Again.

"You're right. You're right. You're RIGHT." And she was right. But here he was, Ron Watson, former playboy...ur, playzombie, formerly not having to give a fuck about anything except where to find his next meal, and now he was a family man...ur, family zombie, with a grown daughter, a newborn son, and a girlfriend he loved as much as his black zombie heart would allow him to love, and...what was wrong with this picture?

Ron knew what was wrong with this picture. He gently released his girlfriend and his son, laid them both down on the bed, and reached up to his face, where a piece of 'Vegas' duct tape resided. He ripped the tape off of his face with one motion, pulling bits of zombie skin and dried blood with it, and carefully fashioned a ring out of the duct tape and zombie skin bits. He then dropped to one knee and, with his left hand, held up the bloody duct tape ring, the V in 'Vegas' showing at the top. "Maria, will you make an honest zombie out of me? Will you be my Forever ZILF?"

The earth froze on its axis a third time and the room grew as heavy as a skyscraper atop a skyscraper atop a third skyscraper. Again. Actually, this time the weight was four skyscrapers, it was that heavy. Finally, after a length of time that made Ron nervous – because he was a man, and pauses in conversations with women always make men nervous – Maria grabbed Ron's right hand, held it to her chest, and spoke, the love in her voice illuminating the room like a nuclear bomb in a New Mexican desert.

"Ron Watson, from the moment I saw you on that plane, I liked you. And from the moment you turned me into a zombie to save my life, I loved you. When will I ever again find a man…ur, zombie, who would do that for me? Never. So my answer is…Brains!"

"Brains!"

"WAAAAAAAAAAH!"

Flippy, his bald head sweaty from serving tourists from every state in the union, his energy high from pounding energy drinks, was tending bar on this lovely December day, and as soon as he saw Ron shamble into Carnaval Court he started laughing.

"You again? What the fuck, Ron? I see you all the time now! Did you move here or something?"

"Yes, Flippy, I did. Remember the woman who was shot here last week?"

"Yeah, hot blonde?"

"Yeah."

"I remember, she was with you."

"She was my fiancee."

"Oh, I'm sorry, man. Let me buy you a drink. Losing your fiancee is tough."

"No, she wasn't my fiancee then, she's my fiancee now."

"You have a dead fiancee – OHHHH. I gotcha. One zombie, coming up!" Flippy turned to make Ron a drink.

"Flippy, I need a job."

"Yeah, we all do, Ronnie boy. Even I know I can't work here forever." Bottles were in the air as Flippy turned to face Ron. "Even with my majestic looks and magnetic smile." He smiled and caught the bottles of alcohol out of the air without spilling a drop.

"Can I work here?"

"Here?" The alcohol was flowing into a cup right in front of Ron, seemingly without the use of hands; it was like being in the front row at a Harry Houdini show.

"Yes, here."

"Can you flair?"

"Throw bottles in the air and make drinks appear in front of people like magic?"

"Yeah. We have an opening for a flair bartender and, frankly -" Flippy leaned over the bar and spoke in a low tone – "you wouldn't want any of the other jobs we have here, trust me." Flippy turned back to the bar and back around again; he had an empty whiskey bottle in his hand, and handed it to Ron over the bar. "Show me what you got."

Ron took the bottle in his left hand. He hadn't realized up until this point that he would be auditioning for this job today; he had hoped maybe they would send him to flair bartending college first, if there was such a thing. Fuck.

He threw the bottle up in the air, it twirled perfectly like a tiny Russian gymnast at the Olympic games and Ron remembered his days as a high school busboy at a family restaurant. It wasn't a 'flair' job per se, but he did have to catch a lot of crap thrown his way, as is the style of a cheap family restaurant on the outskirts of town. The customer base of such a place generally likes to throw things, and Ron learned to catch everything with his right hand.

His right hand.

His RIGHT HAND.

His RIGHT MOTHERFUCKING HAND, WHICH WAS AT-TACHED TO HIS RIGHT MOTHERFUCKING ARM WHICH WAS CURRENTLY INOPERABLE. The bottle fell harmlessly to the rubber floor below the barstools.

Fuck.

"You, uh, might want to get that arm looked at," Flippy said with a smile. "You would need it to work here."

"Yeah, apparently," Ron said, and he took a swig from his drink with his left hand. "Damn." As he drank and realized his career as a flair bartender was over, he pondered what other jobs he could get in his new hometown:

- He could be a pimp, but then he'd want to eat himself on moral grounds and he was pretty sure Cannibal Zombies wasn't the right fucking major for him, either.

- He could be a card slapper, out on the Vegas Strip, trying to entice passing tourists into taking business cards for strippers with names like Debbie Dildo, Cherry Pie, and Martha Stewart (He was pretty sure the Martha Stewart cards would be homemade and have lacy fringe on them). This entails holding business cards with your left hand and, when unsuspecting tourists walk by, slapping the cards twice into your right hand...YOUR RIGHT HAND. Fuck.

- He could be a card dealer in a casino. Nope, scratch that, it would require HIS RIGHT HAND. Fuck.

- He could be a bathroom attendant in a swanky Las Vegas bathroom, offering people paper towels when they were done washing their hands or mints for their breath or whatever. That would only require one hand, right? Then Ron remembered the time he and Jim chased that disgraced politician into the bath-room at Mirage and made an absolute mess eating him....and he shuddered. Nobody should have to clean that up.

Ron took another swig from his drink and decided nobody was going to hire a one-armed zombie for anything worthwhile. Fuck.

CHAPTER
10

Ron – Zombie.
Maria – Mombie.
Stella – Big Sister!
Jim – Zombie, and lovin' it!
Ron Junior – Poopin' diapers, yo!

Sargeant Stedenko – yes, it was his real name, and he was tired of all the Cheech and Chong jokes, thank you very much – had been on the Las Vegas Police Force for 35 years and was retiring this week. Yes, it was true, and he was also tired of all the stereotypical movie trope jokes, thank you very much. Stedenko was a heavy and cranky man; a product of too many Krispy Kreme Donuts, In N Out Burgers, alimony payments to his bitch of an ex-wife, and late nights prowling the alleys behind the casinos on the Las Vegas Strip, looking for hookers or murderers or whatever. Yeah, oftentimes it came down to whatever. Vegas was full of of whatever. In fact, Stedenko has decided that 'Vegas' in Spanish probably meant 'whatever.' Not that he knew; he was speaking English only, dammit, and wished that every motherfucking wetback who crossed over the motherfucking Rio Grande to get into this bastion of freedom we call the U S of motherfucking A would speak English, too. It was our motherfucking language, right? Still, because he was about to retire, whatever. Vegas was full of whatever.

But whatever Vegas was full of, it usually wasn't what Stedenko saw right now. Stedenko had never seen anything like what he saw right now. This was more fucked up than any whatever he could think of. Right now.

"Um, McGarett, Williams (yeah, they were unfortunately named and tired of all the Hawaii 5-0 jokes, too, thank you very much), you better come down here. We have a mess on our hands." Stedenko stopped talking into the walkie-talkie for a moment and threw up on the asphalt of the parking lot of Zombie Island Resort, the newest casino on the Las Vegas Strip. It was brand new and went up quickly; the Middle Eastern conglomerate that owned it knew that the zombie craze was hot and wanted to capitalize on it before the craze moved on. Which, really, doesn't explain how Circus Circus got built (was there ever a circus craze?) but whatever.

Stedenko gathered himself and spoke into his radio again. "And make sure you bring backup. Yeah, I know you're already backup, but we're going to need more backup on top of your backup. It's a mess. Grab everybody you can; Friday, Rockford, Malloy, Reed, Cagney and Lacey, bring 'em all. And body bags. Lots of body bags." He looked at Zombie Island Resort. "And a street sweeper and a bulldozer. The shit has hit the fan."

It certainly appeared that the shit had hit the fan, if the shit was people and the fan was, well, a fan. A giant metal fan with giant metal blades, the kind that, well, chop people up. Stedenko wasn't sure what would be worse; shit or people hitting the fan. 'Cuz right now the people smelled like shit and looked like shit. Somebody – or some *thing* – had taken a shit all over the patrons of the Zombie Island Resort and all that was left was the building...and the body parts inside the building. Stedenko had responded to a call for a code 187, which meant homicide, and he had parked his police car half on the curb of the Vegas strip (cops could do that without Ponch and John hassling them), gotten out of said police car, and barfed. From the smell. Then he ambled his way up the entry sidewalks, past the fake palm trees, beaches and zombies, stuck his head in the front door, and barfed again. From the sight. He then retreated, back to his car, slipping and sliding on his first barf, barfed a third time, and called for backup.

Cagney and Lacey, the backups, pulled up on Segways; they had been just up the block pulling homeless people out of the fountain in front of Caesar's Palace, so they were the first to arrive. And, despite their names, they were men. Fat men. The kind of men who would challenge each other to eat a featured item from each fast food joint in a food court…in the same meal. On a weekly basis. Which Cagney and Lacey did. Some weeks Cagney won (he could slurp a burger faster than you can say "coronary disease") and some weeks Lacey won (he could inhale a piece of pepperoni pizza like he was a Colombian dealer inhaling a line of coke), but every week both of their ample guts won.

And today both of their girthy guts plopped down off the Segways with the bodies carrying them. "I got the call, Sarge," Cagney said, with french fry breath, his Santa Claus gut testing the limits of his XXL police-issued polyester shirt. He stuck his pock-marked nose into the air. "Wow, it smells like shit here."

Lacey had a bean burrito stuffed into his face like a cork trying to plug a leak, so he didn't say anything, but he did stick his misshapen nose into the air and nod his head, as if to say, *yeah, shit.*

All three cops looked towards the casino; Stedenko started walking, but noticed that neither Cagney or Lacey followed him. He got three steps ahead of them and turned around. "Well, you fucking food court junkies, let's go." He walked back to the two frozen cops and jiggled Cagney's belly with his hand. "That must be jelly, 'cuz jam don't shake like that. A walk and a puke will do you good, probably add a good dozen years back onto your shortened life span, even if it's only a walk to the front door of the casino."

"Do we -"

"Do you what, you oversized bag of snickerdoodles?"

"Do we have to?"

Stedenko laughed and shook his head. "Do you have to? Do you have to what? Do you have to do your fucking job?"

"Yes." Lacey had finally finished his bean burrito and could finally smell the odor of human decay coming from the casino. He obviously didn't like it.

"Look, Chiefs Neversalad and Lackofvegetables, I may be retiring this week, but I'm still your fucking Sergeant. Now help me figure out what the fuck happened here or I'll make sure you're on mailroom duty for the rest of your motherfucking careers, you understand?"

"Does that mean…?" Cagney knew what it meant, but he had to ask anyway.

"Yes, dairy queen, it means NO FUCKING SEGWAYS."

You never saw two cops move faster than Cagney and Lacey did. They scurried up the concrete walkways to the front doors of the casino, opened the doors, and threw up. It was like a synchronized swimming routine at the Olympics, except instead of swimming it was barfing and instead of the Olympics it was at the Zombie Island Resort in Las Vegas, Nevada.

"Hello everybody and welcome to the six o'clock news." A vacuous blond newscaster was filling the dinner hour as Stella, Maria, Ron and Jim were having a quiet dinner at Ron and Maria's of Chinese takeout (for Stella) and the remains of an escaped prisoner that Jim had captured a couple of weeks ago. Sure, the prisoner was now reheated and a leftover, but in this new world Maria, Ron and Jim had learned that not all of their meals were going to be fresh. They also learned the value of having a freezer and a microwave.

That's when all hell broke loose. When Ron knew that things were about to change, very much for the worse. When the future of mankind went straight into the shitter. That's right, that's when Ron Junior started crying.

"WAAAAAAAAAAAH!!"

The sound was otherworldly, like an otherworldly Guantanamo Bay prisoner being tortured by making him watch reruns of "Star Search" at half speed and twice volume. Yes, it was that bad.

"In our top story tonight, WAAAAAAAAAH!" Ron wondered why the newscaster on the TV in his apartment was crying like an otherworldly Guantanamo Bay prisoner; it didn't make any sense.

Maria looked up from her Escaped Prisoner Salad with vinaigrette dressing; it wasn't a 'salad' per se, because it didn't have any lettuce…at least, that's how Ron looked at it. How can it be a salad without any lettuce? He knew better than to argue the point, though, because at least they were all eating. And she was his fiancee now; until they were married, he knew he was going to be on his best behavior. He thought he was going to spend the rest of his life on his best behavior, because he truly loved Maria, but he knew that the odds of that happening were lower than the odds of him deciding a salad could not contain lettuce. It was scientific fact, right? People are on their best behavior when they're engaged and once they get married they turn back into their true selves: Neanderthalic slobs who wondered why the fuck your salad didn't have any lettuce.

"Will you help him? I'm still eating my salad. I know you don't think it's a salad, but -"

"It's totally a salad, honey. I can see the kale leaves and the spinach bits right there, between the tricep loin and the ground bicep." Sure, Ron thought he could be on his best behavior for the rest of his life, but the sarcasm was strong with this one.

"Dad!" Stella had a sporkful of Kung Pao Chicken from Las Vegas Fu King in her mouth, but that didn't stop her from berating her father. Hell, nothing stopped her from berating her father these days…but Ron knew that it was all in love, like when a girl in elementary school chases you all over the playground at recess and eventually catches you and beats the fuck out of you, all because she likes you. Not that Ron had any experience with that.

"I'll help him out." Jim had finished his grilled Rack of David (that was presumably the name of the escaped prisoner) and was licking his lips. "I'm done." He got up and went over to Ron Junior, who was sitting in his high chair, a river of spit and First Peas running down his face. Jim looked at the bottle of baby food on the table. "You fed him First Peas? You realize that's also going to be his last peas?"

"You must have fed me First Peas when I was a baby," Stella said. "I fucking hate peas."

"We're live at Zombie Island Resort…" the television was blaring, an audio/visual source of useless information in a room where more important things were happening. "…and it smells like shit."

Ron swallowed his prisoner fingertip. "Whoa. They said *shit* on TV?"

"Dad, they say 'shit' on TV all the time these days. Dumbass." Clearly, Stella was up on the social mores of the day more than her father. *Shit* on TV? Ron shook his head and a flap of his zombie skin went with it. What was this world coming to?

"And a lot of people are dead, according to unconfirmed reports. We'll keep an eye -" the vacuous blonde newscaster was babbling on and on and on, and nobody was paying attention. To the death reports, anyway.

"STELLA! LANGUAGE!" Ron was a new dad, with Ron Jr, and it was affecting his old dad relationship, with Stella. She cussed all the time, and he didn't give a fucking crap, until he had Ron Junior. Now he remembered what it was like to be a parent. "Ron Junior's going to hear you!"

Ron Junior, fortunately or unfortunately, didn't hear her because he was busy choking on First Peas, his tiny airway clogged with lumpy green clumps that were supposed to resemble peas but, legally, were probably processed enough that they didn't qualify as 'food' anymore. It's amazing what we feed ourselves and our fellow human beings these days.

Maria screamed as Stella and Ron looked at each other with wide eyes. Jim was still standing at Ron Junior's high chair and realized that he was choking, so Jim, who was a lifeguard at a San Diego beach in high school, calmly picked Ron Junior up in his arms, flipped him over onto the melamine table, and started hitting Ron Junior in the back, five times.

"WHAT THE FUCK?" Ron asked, as Jim flipped Ron Junior over and gave him five thrusts in his chest.

"Trust me," Jim exclaimed to the frantic room, and flipped Ron Junior over onto his belly. He then gave him five more back blows, which to Ron looked like Jim was beating the fuck out of Ron Junior…but then Ron Junior stopped choking and started crying.

"WAAAAAAAAAAH" Ron Junior exclaimed to the worried adults, and to the adults it sounded like sweet motherfucking relief. A screaming baby is better than a choking baby, for a moment.

And at that moment Maria swore she was never motherfucking buying First Peas again, Ron swore he was going to motherfucking learn CPR, Jim swore he was going to find a woman he could motherfucking have babies with, and Stella? Well, Stella got up from the table, spilling her steamed rice on the melamine table surface, and walked over to Jim.

"Hey, Ron Junior, is my fucking cussing going to fucking turn you into a fucking cussing machine?" Stella giggled the giggle of a proud drunken sister, which she was, minus the drunken, of course. She had only had one glass of bourbon with dinner. Yeah, she wasn't old enough, legally, to drink bourbon, but her flask didn't judge.

"Stella!" Jim's eyes widened to the point where he looked like Japanese Anime Jim. "What the fuck? He almost choked to death!"

"You had it all the way, Jim," she said. "Come here, young Ron Junior!" She took a screaming Ron Watson Junior out of Jim's arms and snuggled him like a revered Amazon Prime package that was just delivered to the front door, and all of a sudden Screaming Ron Watson Junior became Purring Ron Watson Junior. Although Stella had never been a sister before, she was a natural. And she knew what it was like when your dad was a zombie and he fed you First Fucking Peas. She and Ron Junior would always have those things in common.

"There's a lot of blood and body parts and frankly, the stench makes us all want to barf – and I have, three times, so we recommend that everybody stay away from Zombie Island Resort tonight blahblahblahblah -" The blonde newscaster was droning on and on about some bullshit, Ron thought, as he shivered, thanked his lucky stars, gave Maria a deep kiss on the forehead, and cleared the table. As he cleared plates and realized that he was lucky to know Jim (and Jim's CPR) and that this was his family – that everybody he loved in the entire world was right here, in this room – he felt something deep in his black soul that he hadn't felt in a long, long time. A little bit, a tiny bit, a micro slice, of peace. Despite all of the motherfucking circumstances.

And then he watched three minutes of the six o'clock news and realized that peace isn't what he felt at all.

CHAPTER
11

Ron – Zombie.
Maria – Mombie.
Stella – Big Sister!
Jim – Zombie, and lovin' it!
Ron Junior – Poopin' diapers, yo!

Las Vegas can be a cruel town. Many people arrive in Vegas high on the promise of glamour, the mystique of romance, and the allure of wild success, only to end up ground up and spit out, dogfood for the streets, the victim of misfortune, poor rolls of the dice, or Lady Luck taking a vacation. Not everybody can be a winner, right?

But you know who Las Vegas will never spit out? Who will always have an opportunity to reinvent themselves? Who will forever have the chance to be a winner? Former celebrities. Vegas loves former celebrities. They're hungry for attention, cheap to rent for public consumption, and the public usually kinda sorta remembers who they are, so when Mr. and Mrs. Joe Midwest are visiting Vegas and looking for something to do after dinner, they look at the list and kind of recognize a name from their past, see that the show is cheap – until you throw in the two drink minimum – and wallah! Two more suckers for a night with Joe Blow from Your Favorite TV Show When You Were A Kid.

Ron Watson's phone buzzed on a Saturday mid-mornternoon – the lazy, hazy time between morning and afternoon – when he was home trying to rock Ron Junior to sleep. Maria was napping in the bedroom and Ron and Junior were rocking in the LaZboy in front of the TV (turned all the way down) so Junior would (hopefully) fall asleep. It was his nap time, so the little motherfucker should be going to sleep, right? Ron thought so. It was logical, but infants and logic go together like bananas and motor oil sometimes, so Ron Junior was, instead of going to sleep, wailing like a suburban mother being chased by a zombie.

"WAAAAAAAAAAAAHHHHHHHH!" Ron Junior proclaimed with pointed insistence.

"WAAAAAAAAAAAAAHHHHHHHHH!" Ron Senior replied with pointed sarcasm. Fuck it, if the kid wasn't going to fucking sleep when he was fucking supposed to, his dad was going to make fun of him. It was, after all, the job of fathers everywhere to give their kids shit about their stupid shit. Like not going to fucking sleep when it was fucking nap time. And later, about smoking fucking marijuana in the high school bathroom. And further down the line, getting fucking married before they were 40 years old.

His phone buzzed and Ron looked at it. A Las Vegas number. Fuck. It was either Doctor Roberts looking for more Ron Zombie souvenirs – or checking on Ron Junior – or Flippy, wondering when Ron was coming back to the bar to spend some more money because Flippy needed to make a mortgage payment. Or maybe Flippy needed to build another pool at his house. Ron tipped well when he was Carnaval Court, and all the bartenders knew it.

Ron answered his phone, because at the moment he'd rather talk to any adult than to Ron Junior, whose vocabulary consisted of one word. "WAAAAAAAAAAAAHHHHHHHH."

"Hello?"

"Hey Ron. Dave." A voice, unrecognizable.

"Um, Dave's not here." Ron Junior stopped wailing and giggled.

"No, I'm Dave."

"Dave?"

"Yeah."

"Dave's not here." Ron Junior giggled again, his belly jiggling like fresh jello.

"No, I'm Dave."

"Dave's not here." Ron realized he was borrowing an old Cheech and Chong routine, but every time he said 'Dave's not here,' his son giggled. And every parent knows that when you do something that makes your wailing offspring giggle, you keep doing it and you overdo it until you've overdone it so much that it makes your offspring wail again. Rule #52 of parenting.

Five minutes later Ron Junior was wailing again, the voice on the phone was irritated, and Ron was still laughing. He never knew when a joke was over.

"RON, IT'S DAVE, YOUR AGENT!"

"Oh, THAT Dave!"

"YOU hired me!"

"Sorry, Dave. Just making my baby laugh."

"Sounds like your baby is crying, Ron."

"He was laughing a minute ago."

"Right. Listen, I have a job for you."

Um, shit, Ron thought. A job? Sure, he thought he wanted a job, because Maria did ask him to get one, but did he really want a job? A *job* job? Like, something that took actual work? Ron hadn't had a job since he became a zombie, and, truth be told, he found joblessness to be one of the more positive aspects of being a zombie. Face it: nobody would work if they didn't have to. If they weren't being paid to. And besides, he only had one arm. And was a zombie. Who the fuck was going to hire him?

"What kind of job?" Ron could taste the bile rise up in his stomach. A *job*. Ugh. The only job he really wanted, outside of eating people and stealing their money, was flair bartending at Carnaval Court with his friends, but that obviously wasn't going to happen until he learned how to flair bartend. And got a new right arm. Somehow.

"My client want you to DJ a dayclub."

Ron thought for a second and realized he wasn't sure what that meant. "Hee hay a who what?"

"DJ a dayclub. You know, play music for all the 20-somethings in the pool. A lot of former celebrities do it."

Ron looked down at Ron Junior, who was clad in a 'Ron Zombie went to Vegas and all he got me was this lousy onesie' onesie, was done sobbing, and was now looking up at Ron as if though he was ready to play 'Where's Dave' again. Ron smiled at him and asked Dave the most obvious question. "I'm a *former* celebrity now?"

"Zombies are out, Ron. As of 11:11am yesterday."

"Wow, you guys really have it down to the minute?"

"Khloe Kardashian – maybe it was Kim – or maybe it was Karma, I can never keep them straight – tweeted a picture of her new werewolf buddy to the world and everything changed. At 11:11am yesterday. Nobody gives a shit about zombies anymore."

"And ZTV?" Somebody had started a new TV channel just for zombies called ZTV; it was Ron's favorite channel. Cooking shows featuring human flesh, 'Survivor' type shows featuring humans being chased by zombies, and missing person shows where Ron knew the people who had been eaten…because he had eaten them.

"Off the air. Since 11:12am yesterday."

"Fuck." Ron sighed. The more things change, the more they fucking change, apparently.

"They'll pay you to DJ the dayclub, Ron. four hours of work for a thousand dollars."

"That was my favorite TV cha – wait, what?" Did he say a thousand dollars?

"Four hours of work. One thousand dollars."

Ron Junior started to fall sleep, FINALLY. Ron looked at him and saw how beautiful he was. How innocent. How sweet. How expensive.

"I'll do it."

"Great, Ron. Be at the Harrah's pool by 11am Saturday morning for check in, and they'll get you set up. You'll spin from noon to six, with regular breaks."

"Um, wait. One question."

"Yes?" Dave sounded slightly agitated, and Ron really wanted this gig – well, no, he didn't want this gig, he wanted this money, but that meant taking this gig – so he didn't want to upset Dave, but at the same time this next question was rather important, so fuck it.

"Spin? Do I actually have to spin records?" Ron wondered if a one-armed zombie with no experience could actually spin records. Then a bigger, more nightmarish thought entered his black mind. "Do I have to bring my own records?" Shit, Ron realized, his mom gave away his records when he went off to college. It sure would be nice to still have Foreigner 4, the Thompson Twins, and Motley Crue's first record; Ron was sure the kids would like those. Fuck, he would have to go to a used record shop before the gig and restock.

"No, Ron. We know you have a bum arm, first of all. And second of all, DJing these days is all about pushing the 'play' button on a laptop and letting the previously set-up play list play through."

"Oh, so 'I Wanna Know What Love Is' is already programmed into the machine? And 'We Built This City?'"

Dave laughed and cleared his throat. "Um, just show up, Ron. They'll pick out music for you. These days the kids all want to hear EDM when they're at the pool."

EDM? What the fuck? Elephant Dong Music? Electric Delicatessen Movements? Esoteric Doctor Masturbations?

"Electronic Dance Music, Ron." Clearly Dave could intuitively tell that Ron had no idea what EDM was. It was either that or the long pause in the conversation gave it away.

"Oh, like Depeche Mode."

"Not quite, Ron. Just show up."

Ron had never done anything like this, but it was a job, so Ron, who was always a good employee, did as he was told and showed up.

First, however, Maria packed Ron a lunch – Frank Dip, featuring meat from Frank, a convicted murderer, on a hoagie roll from Safeway, with a side of blood, also from Frank – and then Ron showed up on time, wearing a "Ron Zombie" t-shirt, because he figured if they were hiring him because of who he was, he should remind everybody who he was. It was his show, right?

Except it wasn't. Because when he got to Harrah's, there was a sign above the DJ station next to the pool.

"Monster Jam Saturday featuring Liam the Werewolf!" And, in smaller letters, "with Ron Zombie."

Wait, what? Had Ron really fallen far enough from his celebrity perch that a fucking werewolf was ahead of him in the celebrity pecking order? Was he now a – egad! – a second tier celebrity? A third tier celebrity? A Dustin Diamond? A Lindsey Lohan? A – egad! – William Hung?

"Hey, pardner," he said, to the first Harrah's employee he saw. He called him 'Pardner' because he didn't see his name tag that said 'Anthony,' and 'pardner' was Ron's generic greeting to just about anybody whose name tag he didn't see.

"Yeah?" Anthony replied, his name tag in full view of Ron's eyes, his burly hipster beard blotting out the sun. At least it felt that way. Ron wondered why every young dude on the planet wanted to look like a lumberjack these days.

"Oh, sorry, Anthony. Hey, I'm Ron Zombie. Who is Liam the Werewolf? And why does he have top billing today?"

"Who?"

"Liam the Werewolf?"

"Oh, I know who Liam is. Who did you say you were?"

Ron took a deep breath and pondered how he could justify eating a Harrah's employee. Specifically a bearded, hipster Harrah's employee named 'Anthony.' He realized he needed to invent an app for zombies that would allow them to run quick background checks on potential meals on their phones. Everybody has skeletons in their closet, right? Surely this Anthony had done something in his past to justify Ron eating him here and now.

"Ever been in jail, Anthony?"

"No, sir." Anthony's eyes grew suspicious, but his beard did not. It still hung out happily in the Vegas air, not a care in the world, like a douchebag's plumage. At least Ron assumed Anthony was a douchebag. Given the muttonchops growing below Anthony's chin, Ron felt it was a fair assumption. Or, perhaps, just maybe, Ron was a little old to understand the lives of the young. Nah, fuck that shit.

"Ever should have been in jail, Anthony? Like maybe you killed somebody but didn't tell anybody?"

"No, sir. Who are you again? Do I need to get my manager?" Ah, fuck, Ron thought, Anthony was just an innocent kid working for the man, despite his lumberjack face.

"No, Anthony, you don't need to. I'm Ron Zombie. I'm second -" Ron threw up in his mouth a little bit - "billed today. Apparently."

"Oh, Mister Zombie, of course! You're that guy who was famous until yesterday!"

"Yep, that's me."

Anthony stuck his hand out. "Pleased to meet you, sir."

"You can stop calling me sir, Anthony. Ron will suffice."

"Will what, sir?"

"Just call me Ron."

"Okay, Ron. Your DJ booth is right over there." Anthony pointed to a spot right next to the deep end of the pool where a canopy was set up.

"Oh, cool, thanks, Anthony."

"You're welcome, si – uh, Mister Zombie."

"Ron."

"Whatevs."

Whatevs? Ron smirked and wondered how young people ever passed English class these days. Whatevs. Totes. It was ridic...or maybe Ron was just jelly.

Ron ambled over to his DJ booth and was pretty impressed with it, initially. A little fridge filled with water bottles, a canopy overhead to protect him from the hot Vegas sun, a chair, and a table with a laptop on it. *Just push play*, a sticker on the laptop said. It was pretty impressive...until Ron looked across the pool to the shallow end and saw a much bigger booth – probably four times as big – with the words 'LIAM THE WEREWOLF' in neon lights above the booth. And four girls in skimpy string bikinis in the booth. And giant champagne buckets each side of the stage, filled with ice and oversized bottles of Moet & Chandon.

And fireworks.

Fucking fireworks.

Ron looked up; yep, they were shooting off fireworks from Liam's booth. Ron looked down; his booth had no fireworks. Or champagne. Or bikinis.

What.

The.

Fuck.

Ron shuffled over to Liam's booth on the shallow end of the pool. Fuck it, he was calling it a palatial estate now, because that's what it was compared to Ron's mobile home of a booth. At the palatial estate booth, another lumberjack hipster was drinking champagne and talking to two girls in bikinis with the tops made with the word 'Liam' on one breast and the word 'Werewolf' on the other while a team of Harrah's employees scurried around, checking wires and connections and fireworks.

"The fireworks are ready," one said into a walkie-talkie.

"The laptop is ready," another said into a different walkie-talkie.

"The champagne is cold," a third said.

Damn, Ron thought, all I have is a fucking city arts fair folding canopy; this Liam character got all the good stuff. He wondered if jealousy was enough of a reason to eat Harrah's employees.

"And you are?" The lumberjack hipster, dressed in a collared blue club shirt and white linen pants, was now talking to Ron.

"Oh, I'm Ron Zombie. I'm the deep end DJ today, apparently. Is Liam around? I'd like to meet him."

"You just did."

Ron looked around; he didn't remember meeting a werewolf recently. Or ever.

"What?"

"I'm Liam."

Ron stepped back. He sure had a lot of hair on his face. He was just a hipster, right?

"The Werewolf," Liam continued.

"I've heard of you," Ron replied. "But aren't you just a hipster? Are you really a werewolf?"

"Well," Liam said, a smile on his face, "I clean up well. But yes, I'm a werewolf. Have you not seen my t-shirts everywhere?" Liam turned, reached into a box behind him, and pulled out a large t-shirt with Liam's face emblazoned across the front of it. "Here."

Ron took the shirt and noticed that Liam's hands were also quite hairy. He then pointed at his own Ron Zombie t-shirt. "Thanks, but I have this."

"Oh," Liam said, "That's cute. But you're required to wear my shirt when you're DJing with me. It's part of the deal."

"There's a deal?"

"Yeah, I'm a headlining DJ and during my 15 minute breaks every hour you're the DJ. And you're wearing my t-shirt. It's in your contract."

"I didn't get a contract. Just a phone call."

"Oh, that's right, Dustin Diamond backed out. Sorry, you were a last minute replacement. Glad you're here, whoever you are!" Liam slapped Ron on the back and walked away and Ron realized he had never felt so alone in all of his time as a zombie.

And for the rest of the day Ron hung out for 45 minutes while the shallow end of the pool was filled with scantily clad 20-some-things partying their young asses off with Liam the Werewolf DJ. Telling werewolf jokes ("Where does a werewolf sit?" "Anywhere it wants to!"), combing their faces with officially licensed 'Liam The DJ' combs, and howling at the sun.

And then Ron pushed 'play' on his laptop for 15 minutes while nobody partied. Have you ever tried to party in the deep end of a pool?

CHAPTER
12

Ron – Unemployed.
Maria – Mombie.
Stella – Teenager.
Jim – Zombie and lovin' it!
Ron Junior – Toddler

Celebrity, in theory, is fleeting, although you apparently can't tell the Kardashian sisters that, because they're fucking still around and nobody fucking knows why. However, in most instances, celebrity shows up at your door, takes a walk through your house, adds onto your house and buys you some nice things, makes your face recognizable to everybody on the planet who's paying attention, and then walks out, taking fame with it, turning you into a fame whore who wonders why nobody gives a shit about you anymore…Kardashian sisters notwithstanding.

Ronald James Watson was this generation's Tonya Harding. Okay, this year's Tonya Harding. Okay, this week's Tonya Harding. Yeah, fame fucked him and walked out, not leaving even a penny on the nightstand. She was a harsh mistress, at best, as Ron had learned from the whole DJ experience.

Ron wandered into Carnaval Court on a Monday as the bartender Rob, his taut tattooed Asian arms glistening with sweat and a twenty-dollar bill stuck to his brown forehead, finished pouring free shots at the bar for the gathered throng of thirsty tourists and regular alcoholics. Rob saw Ron and his mouth fell into a grin as wide as the gulf between Las Vegas gambling expectations and Las Vegas gambling reality.

"Ron, my motherfucking man, how's it hanging?" Rob had his hand in the air to give Ron a high-five, which Ron returned with his left hand, because his stupid right hand wasn't working. Stupid right hand.

"Rob, have you noticed anything…different?"

"Different, my man? You mean like the special on Bacardi we're running right now?" Rob grabbed a bottle of Bacardi and threw it in the air.

"No, different different."

"You mean like when you're in high school and a girl likes you and then she *likes* you likes you?" The bottle of Bacardi landed in Rob's right hand as softly as a cotton ball landing on another cotton ball.

"Yeah, that kind of different different."

Rob pushed a drink across the bar to Ron. "Here, I made this for you. On the house."

"On the house?"

"On the motherfucking house, Ron, my man."

Ron paused; a drink on the house at Carnaval Court was as rare as a cotton ball landing on top of another cotton ball. What. The. Fuck?

"Okaaaaaaaay." It was, in the pantheon of 'okays', the third official kind of 'okay'. The first is the normal 'okay', which is to say, a*lright, I agree with what you just said.* The second is the far more normal sarcastic, "OKAY!" which is to say, *God, lay the fuck off! I'll take the fucking trash out!* And the third? Well, that was this. "Okaaaaaaay," which is to say, *I don't think this is a very good idea, personally, and I'm quite wary of the consequences of your upcoming* *actions, but for some stupid fucking reason – I could be drunk, or I could be smitten, or I could just be wary of confrontation – I'm going to go along with it. Probably.* That's what this okay was.

"Ron," Rob looked around at the gathered crowd, which this day consisted of three friends of the bartenders, seven drunk tourists from the Midwest, and eleven people who were all friends with 'Joyce,' who was turning 40, according to her sash and tiara. Brave girl, Joyce, announcing her real age. Ron wondered why she didn't lie like everybody else on their birthday. With dark shoulder length hair, brown skin, and a sweet body, she looked like she might have been 30. Might have.

"Ron, I get it."

"You get what?"

"You're not IN anymore."

"In?"

"Isn't that what you were talking about?"

"No, I was talking about the zombies."

"I'm talking about werewolves."

"Oh. Fuck werewolves," Ron replied.

"Zombies are so last week, Ron."

Ron took a sip of his drink. Bacardi and 7Up, not his favorite, but when it's on the house…

"Last week?"

"Yeah. Werewolves are this week."

"This week, last week, whatthefuckever. Fuck werewolves. What about the bodies? What about the killer zombies on the loose?"

"Whoa, Ron, I know you're upset about being last week's news, but -"

"Rob, there are zombies who are killing people. Have you seen the news?"

"Ronnie, that's what zombies do. We all know the story; brains, eating, blahblah. Last week's news. Now everybody's trying to grow all their hair out so they can look like werewolves! That's *this* week's news! Tell you what, I'll put some antidote in your next drink and you can be human and laugh at werewolves with us."

Ron laughed. "Antidote – you're funny. We all know that's not real."

The bartender Charlie came around the bend in the circular bar, his boyish face and brown mop-top hair complementing his scene-stealing grin, but not the fake mutton-chop that he had obviously glued to his face. "Check it out, bitches! I'm a motherfucking werewolf!" He lifted his hands in the air and danced around the area behind the bar like a circus clown who was the offspring of an uncoordinated stripper. Ron laughed; Charlie was clearly a man who lived life without any fucks to give. It was an admirable trait, Ron thought. If he had no fucks to give, he wouldn't be worried about zombies right now. And if Ron were an algebra teacher, he'd present this equation as *0 fucks = happiness.*

"See? If Charlie knows about it, it must be the latest damn thing," Rob said. "I don't get it, but I didn't get the zombie thing either." A customer sidled up next to Ron to order a drink and Rob moved three feet to his left to take the order.

"Charlie, zombies are killing people." Ron looked at Charlie, who resembled a hipster who didn't know how to use a glue gun, and giggled. He couldn't help it.

"Oh, fuck you, Ron. You're still talking about zombies? Everybody knows motherfucking werewolves are where it's at!" He danced again and Ron broke out into a full throttle laugh. A man like Charlie, who lived on his own terms and didn't care what your terms were, was a delight to know, seriously. Even when he wasn't taking you seriously.

"But I'm Ron Watson. Zombie."

Charlie danced back around to face Ron. "We know who you are, Ronnie. You've been coming here for years."

Ron looked up at the stage, where The Whipits were on a break and a DJ was playing a techno mashup of "The Humpty Dance" and "Rhiannon," which pretty much made Ron's ears bleed. He liked "The Humpty Dance" but Stevie Nicks' voice was, to Ron, like somebody using a jackhammer in his eardrum. Like somebody forcing him to watch an every Kevin Costner movie, consecutively, in one sitting. Like having to sit through political ads after you've voted by mail already.

Who the fuck would mash up anything with Stevie Nicks' voice?

Who the fuck would look up to a werewolf?

Who the fuck would think that Ron Watson was not *in*?

Ron finished his drink and left Carnaval Court feeling like this world no longer had a place for him.

CHAPTER
13

Ron – Zombie.
Maria – Mombie.
Stella – Chemist.
Jim – Zombie and lovin' it!
Ron Junior – Toddler.

Vegas Valley View Junior College is like everything else in Las Vegas: fake and in the desert. Sure, it looked like Harvard, but like all the best Vegas hotels, it was 'fakeitecture.' All facade, none of it real. Sure, it was a real junior college, but it looked like Harvard. And it wasn't Harvard, obviously. It was a junior college in Las Vegas. Big difference.

Stella was a student at VVVJC only because her dad told her it was a stepping stone to Harvard and a career and a better life. She couldn't imagine a better life than hanging out with her zombie father all the time and hiding her zombie friends from the authorities all the time, but that was a sarcastic thought and yes, she could imagine a better life, actually. So she went. Secretly she hoped to become a lawyer one day and fight for zombie rights and that would be her better life, but she would never tell her dad that, because she was still a teenager and still a rebel and still could never let her father know that he was right. It wasn't the teenager thing to say. Going because your dad MADE you go was the teenager thing to say. Fuck him and his fucking rules....outwardly. Inwardly, become a lawyer and fight for zombie rights.

So she went.

And she studied chemistry, although she told Ron she was studying psychology. She didn't want him to catch on to what she was was trying to do, because if it worked it would change everything and she wasn't sure her dad liked change. No, in fact, she was sure he didn't like change. When the family's local Safeway turned into a Von's, Ron was beside himself for a few days. Not literally, because being beside yourself is literally impossible unless you or your beside self is a wax figure or something. Stella always thought it would be cool to be famous enough to have a wax figure of yourself in some wax museum somewhere so she could go visit and be literally beside herself.

But, for the moment, Stella was a student at VVVJC and, in her Advanced Chemistry Class (she tested out of the beginning chemistry class because she was very, very good at chemistry), she recreated the zombie antidote that she and some friends had stumbled upon in high school. It was a fluke result that was not entirely unexpected from a gang of smart, latchkey, mischievous teenagers with a bunch of after-school time on their hands. And with a 24 hour convenience store across the street from the high school. And an animal rendering plant down the street. And a weed dealer around the corner. Yeah, sometimes you get high and start mixing weird shit together when you're a teenage chemistry geek.

And remembering how that all came together sounds difficult, but Stella had a mind like a Thought Roach Motel: Thoughts can check in but they can't check out. So she remembered everything about it, and when she became a student at VVVJC under her dad's "orders," she immediately enrolled in a chemistry class and set about recreating the antidote. Sure, she had to add a pint of yak blood, an old piece of 'Garbage Pail Kids' gum, and a jar of Nutella (it was the secret ingredient) to each gallon of antidote, but these days you can find anything on the internet. Even Nutella.

After successfully recreating the antidote in her Advanced Chemistry Class and successfully re-animating a tiny piece of dead human tissue for her professor (she didn't want her professor to know what she was really up to) to get an 'A' grade, Stella loaded up the barrel of antidote she had been hiding in the teacher's lounge (nobody ever goes in there) into her El Camino and took it to the Ring of Foreclosure to test it. It was the perfect experimental group, and really, there was no need for a control group (the group that receives placebos in a scientific test), because they were all zombies, right? If the antidote didn't work, what's the worst that could happen? They could die? No, the worst that could happen would be that they would remain zombies, duh. It was a win/win for everybody. Or a lose/lose, depending on your viewpoint.

The first test subject to receive the antidote was Bob, because he and Stella had gotten along swimmingly whilst he was a zombie. He was a shitty pool player and she kicked his ass at eight ball pretty regularly, but the truth was that Stella had never met a zombie that could put a striped ball in the corner pocket to save his life. So to speak. But Bob seemed like a guy who might enjoy being alive, so Stella called Flippy over – the antidote only worked if a bartender from Carnaval Court administered it, specifically Flippy – and Flippy poured fresh antidote down Bob's throat while standing on a table above him.

20 minutes later, give or take, after Flippy had left and while Stella was doing the dishes in the kitchen at 2087 Forest Lane Drive, a new two story stucco McMansion that she dubbed 'Casa De Zombie,' she heard a voice behind her. "Stella?" She turned around and there was a guy standing there in khaki pants, a blue polo shirt, and boat shoes. He could have been a businessman, a father, or a volunteer coach, but he sure as shit wasn't a zombie.

"Bob?"

"Stella?"

"BOB?"

"STELLA?"

Stella walked over and gave Bob a bear hug, like a sister hugging her big brother just before he goes off to college. She looked him over; his skin was as fresh as the morning dew, he didn't stink (as much as he formerly did, anyway – he was a guy, after all, so he always stunk somewhat) and, more importantly, when she touched his face it stayed intact. No cheekdrop, which was the term Stella invented for when she touched a zombie's cheek and half of it came off in her hand.

"Fuckin' A, Bob, you're a human!"

"I know! What the fuck?"

"I – well, Flippy – gave you the antidote, Bob," Stella said, her face flush with tears. Most people might not think this was a cryable moment, but Stella had spent a lot of time with these zombies and they were good people. Zombies. Whatever they were, they deserved a chance to be human again. She welled up. "And I'm not crying, motherfucker, it's just raining on my face."

Bob hugged her tightly, her tears absorbed into his polo shirt like a sadness sponge, although these weren't tears of sadness. "It's okay, honey, your eyeballs are just sweaty."

"I was cutting onions."

"Fuck onions," Bob said, as they stood there, next to the granite island in the suburban kitchen in the Ring of Foreclosure on the outskirts of Las Vegas, and hugged like they were in heaven.

Bob stepped back. "I even took a shower, Stella. A SHOWER! Do you know how good a shower feels after you've been stinky and bloody all this time?" Bob smiled like a child; even his teeth looked new!

Stella wiped her tears on the tail of his polo. "I don't, but I can imagine. And where'd you get those clothes, Bob? You look like a fucking real estate agent!"

"There's a whole closet full of them upstairs!" Bob looked down at his polo; stitched on the breast was the word 'Bob.' "I guess I picked the right one!"

And with that, Stella single-handedly started the real estate renaissance on the outskirts of Las Vegas.

CHAPTER
14

Ron – Unfamous Zombie.
Maria – Mombie.
Stella – Teenager.
Jim – Zombie.
Ron Junior – Toddler.

In America, a celebrity is never really washed up. Sure, they might fall from first-tier celebrity status, where they can make $20 million in a weekend hawking their latest movie/sextape/ political view, but there's always second-tier celebrity status, where they can make $10 million in a month wearing nothing at an awards show or talking shit about Taylor Swift on Twitter. Or there's twentieth-tier celebrity status, where they can make a few thousand in a weekend embarrassing themselves on 'reality' TV…. which, despite the name, is neither reality, nor is it good TV. Who the fuck decided that watching beautifully plastic people go about their beautifully unrealistic daily 'lives' is interesting?

Ron Watson had fallen to seventieth-tier celebrity status, it felt like, after discovering that fucking hipsters…ur, werewolves, were the next big thing. Not even 'next,' really – they were *now* the big thing. And the more people gave a shit about werewolves, the less of a shit they gave about zombies. It was almost like the world was full of shit, but only enough shit to give to one fad at a time. Thus, werewolves. Or hipsters. Or werewolves.

And Ron Watson, Lord of the Zombies, was feeling it, ever since the infamous DJ gig and Monday at Carnaval Court. Fucking werewolves were stealing his mojo, his thunder, and his lightning. Hell, he was pretty sure he even saw some bums behind The Venetian wearing Ron Zombie shirts. It seemed like just a couple of weeks ago every 25-year-old douchebag party hipster in Vegas was wearing one! If the bums were wearing them...he shuddered. The meteoric rise and the meteoric fall of the greatest zombie of all time. OF ALL TIME. He was pretty sure if there were an award for GZOAT and they tried to award it to somebody else, Kanye West would interrupt the speech. "I'ma let you finish, but Ron Watson is the greatest zombie of all time!"

So when Dave, Ron's agent, called on a random Tuesday, Ron happily answered. He hadn't heard from the fucker in a long time...well, really, it hadn't been that long, but still. Any amount of time is a long time in the fleeting world of celebrity-ism when you're falling faster than Thelma and Louise in a car at the end of a movie. So Ron answered the call. He didn't want to get a real job; hopefully Dave had something for him that could delay that. And something better than being a fucking relief DJ to a fucking hipsterwolf. And something that could make him famous again.

"Got something for you, Ronnie."

"Yeah, Dave? Whatcha got?" Ron slurped up the last blood from the bowl in front of him; who knew that serial killers could taste so good?

"Something that's gonna make you a lotta money, Ron."

"Yeah, Dave?" Ron licked his lips; they were salty, in a very bloody-lusty sort of way. He thought he tasted sea salt and vinegar.

"And make you famous again; put you back on the map."

The map. Ron pondered this for a second; everybody always said 'back on the map,' but was there really a map? Did celebrities posses some magical map that showed the exact road leading from wherever they were back to stardom? Is that how Robert Downey Jr. got his second chance? Did Ron actually already need a second chance? Fuck.

"Am I off the map, Dave?"

"Werewolves, Ron. Or hipsters. It's hard to tell sometimes."

"Fuck. Yeah, I know. So whatcha got?"

"Reality TV, Ron."

Ron squinted his eyes; reality TV? Where nothing was real? The professional wrestling of television?

"I thought ZTV went off the air?"

"It did, Ron, but now there's a new channel."

"What? YTV? WTV?"

"RTV. Reality Television. Only reality shows."

"Wow. That sounds awful."

"It is, but they need content. So they want to do 'Keeping up with the Watsons,' using your whole family. You know, zombie parents don't understand human kids, human kids don't understand zombie parents, blahblahblah...it'd make for great TV, Ron!"

"Would it put me back on the map, Dave?"

"Ever heard of the Kardashians, Ron?"

"Who the fuck hasn't?"

"Exactly. And what have they done?"

"A sex tape."

"You already have your sex tape, Ron."

"Wait, what?"

"Not literally, dumbass, but people already know who you are. Your first round of fame was your sex tape. Now it's time for you to get back on the map with a reality TV show, like the Kardashians."

"I like the idea of being back on the map, Dave, but -"

"I'm not done, Ron. There's a competing company who wants to follow Stella around at the junior college, documenting her life, and they'll call it 'My Dad's A Zombie.'"

"No -"

"Wait, let me finish. There's another company out of LA who wants to follow Maria around and create a show called, 'The Real Housewife of Ron Zombie.'"

"Holy fuck."

"And the folks behind 'Deadliest Catch' want to do a spinoff showing how you get your meals."

"You're a hell of an agent, Dave."

"And, finally, HGTV wants to do a show called 'Fix It Or Zombie It,' where they bring you somebody who's dying and you get to decide whether to let them die or to bite them and turn them into a zombie."

Ron bent over at his waist and threw up into his kitchen sink. He wiped his mouth with a paper towel and took a swig of water. "Dave, that's a little extreme, don't ya think?"

"Yeah, Ronnie, maybe you're right. Maybe that one's better for Showtime."

CHAPTER
15

Ron – Engaged zombie with a hall pass.
Maria – Mombie.
Stella – Teenager.
Jim – Zombie.
Ron Junior – Toddler.

Ron ambled up to the bar as soon as it opened at 1:00, taking his usual spot on a plastic barstool on the south side of the bar. He had a 'hall pass' from Maria for a couple of hours; he had never understood the concept of a 'hall pass' before and, in fact, had often made fun of his married friends who had to get 'hall passes' from their wives, but now that he was engaged to be married to the lovely Maria and had a new baby, he got it. He finally got it. Responsibility sets in if you're not careful. And when that happens, when responsibility sets in and starts kicking your ass with diaper changes and baby poop and job searches and reality television show decisions, you need an occasional 'hall pass' so you can go remind yourself who you are at the core and not have to worry about those things for a little while. Ron knew that the 'hall pass' and hanging out at Carnaval Court made him happy, and he thought that the happier he was, the better boyfriend/father he might be able to be. Might. He still wasn't sure this whole zombie/human/dad existence was all going to be okay in the long run, but he was willing to give it a shot. Hell, there was a Ron Junior now. That was enough reason to soldier on…with the occasional hall pass for well-being. Cheaper than therapy and a helluva lot more fun.

"Ron, my main motherfuckin' man!" Charlie the bartender was doing a dance behind the bar that looked like a mashup between the 'Macarena' and 'Who Let The Dogs Out.' It was early in the day and Charlie was obviously bored, and when Charlie gets bored, he dances. At first it's bizarre but after you've seen it a few times it's just Charlie.

"Carlos!"

"What are ya drinkin' today, Ronnie Ronnerstein?"

"The usual, Sir Charles!" Ron and Charlie high-fived across the bar and Ron felt a warmth inside him that could only come from a hall pass and being able to order 'the usual' at his favorite bar. Either that or he had peed his pants. He looked down; nope, it was from the bar.

As bottles flew into the air and Ron's Manhattan was mixing almost invisibly, a man dressed all in black sat on the bar stool on his left and another man dressed all in black sat on the bar stool on his right. Ron looked to his left; douchebag sunglasses. He looked to his right; douchebag sunglasses. Both dressed all in black on a warm Vegas winter morning that was only going to get warmer. This couldn't be good.

His Manhattan appeared in front of him and Charlie eyed the two military-looking men on either side of Ron. "What will you gentlemen -" Charlie smirked as only Charlie could, like a child about tell his younger brother he saw his parents having sex – "be having?"

"Coors Light," the man on Ron's left replied. Ron would refer to him as Tweedle Dee in his head.

"Coors Light," the man on Ron's right replied. Ron would refer to him as Tweedle Dum in his head.

Ron took a swig of his drink and considered his options. He was hungry all the time these days – he wasn't eating as much due to his newly 'responsible' ways or busy schedule or whatever – so his first option was simple. He was going to eat them both. It would like ordering a double-double at In N Out. Two of everything, please! He licked his zombie lips. Two tibias? Two quadriceps? The snozzberries taste like snozzberries!

But what were their crimes? Ron's conscience asked. It always showed up at the worst time and he wanted to fucking kill it and eat it, too. "You're my dessert," he said out loud to his conscience.

"What, Ronnie boy?"

"Sorry, Charlie, I was thinking of…things."

Charlie smiled and started dancing something that looked like the Hustle, the Bump, and the Electric Slide all rolled in one ridiculous dance casserole. As that casserole circled around to the other side of the bar, Ron's conscience kept fucking talking.

You can't just eat them for no reason, bitch. Yeah, Ron's conscience had taken to calling him bitch; they had a love/hate relationship. Mostly a hate/hate relationship these days, because Ron was *very* hungry all the fucking time. And the only thing stopping him from eating every person in sight? His stupid conscience. But wait, wasn't drinking bad beer reason enough to eat somebody?

No, bitch.

Fuck you, conscience.

Tweedle Dee turned to his right and lowered his douchebag sunglasses. "Mister Watson?"

Ron rolled his eyes to his left without turning his head and eyed the man. You're dressed all in black, you know my name, and you have shitty taste in alcohol; three strikes, I'm going to eat you.

No, you're not. Bitch. Dammit, Ron thought, and shook his head. If I chop off my own head will I get rid of my fucking conscience? *Yes, bitch, but if you chop off your own head you won't be able to eat!* He took his left hand, balled it up into a fist, and hit himself hard in his own face.

Tweedle Dum turned to his left. "You're not Mister Watson?"

Ron rolled his eyes to his right without turning his head and sighed. "What the fuck do you two assbags want?"

Tweedle Dee took a sip of his Coors Light and spoke. "Mister Watson, we need your help."

"Who are you guys?"

Tweedle Dum pulled out his wallet and flashed a badge at Ron. A KILLZ badge. Weren't those fuckers out of business? At the same time Tweedle Dee flashed a gun in Ron's face. A big gun.

Okay, bitch, you can eat these guys. Wow, conscience, thanks a lot. A little late, aren't you? Ron realized he should trust his gut more than his stupid conscience. His gut told him he could eat these guys as soon as they sat down.

Ron took a long swig of his Manhattan and considered the possibilities. He was on a three-hour hall pass at his favorite bar in the entire world and here were his mortal enemies sitting next to him simultaneously asking for his help and threatening his life. This wasn't going to get interesting; it already was.

"Let's go somewhere we can talk." Tweedle Dum looked around the bar like it was bugged with listening devices.

"This is where we talk," Ron said. "Or we don't talk." Ron knew that if he went with these guys to a private location, one of two things would happen: Either he'd end up dead or they'd end up in his stomach. And, frankly, if he couldn't guarantee #2 he didn't want to take a chance on #1. Simple survival, no matter how fucking hungry he was.

Tweedle Dee flashed his gun again. "Mister Watson -"

Charlie danced over like he was a puppet on a string, his perfectly coiffed mop of hair dancing along with him. How the fuck did that guy and his hair know so many dances? "You guys doing alright over here? Ron, do you *neeeeeeed* anything?" Charlie smirked again, like a child about to tell his younger brother that he saw his mom in a porn movie.

"We talk here or we don't talk," Ron said to Tweedle Mother-fucker. He had lost track of who was who. "Do you really want to rile these people up? Remember what happened last time?" Ron motioned around the bar, which was now full of tourists from all over the place. Or maybe they were zombies from all over the place. Ron wasn't sure and didn't care; to KILLZ they were scary either way.

Maybe these KILLZ morons didn't remember last time, Ron thought. Maybe they didn't remember when they showed up at Carnaval Court and were stood down by the gathered throng, all of whom were armed. Or, more likely, maybe Tweedle Dee and Tweedle Dum weren't part of the organization then. Ron knew that KILLZ had a very high turnover rate and an easy application process; hell, he got in when he was a human, right?

Tweedle Dee put his gun back into the waistband of his government-issue black pants, took a swig of his swill, ur, Coors Light – how the fuck is that a 'banquet' beer, Ron wondered – and spoke. "Mister Watson, the zombies are out of hand."

"Wow," Ron said. "You noticed? Observant fuckers, aren't you?"

"Yes, and we need your help." Ron's attempt at sarcasm was obviously way above this guy's pay grade.

"I don't kill zombies," Ron said, and took a sip of his Manhattan. Damn, Charlie made a good Manhattan. "They're my brothers and sisters."

Damn straight, bitch, they're your brothers and sisters. And you'd kill them, but not for these fucks.

"We don't need you to kill them," Tweedle Dum said, his face like that of a teacher admonishing a kindergartner for peeing on the wall in the teacher's lounge, "we need you to change them."

"What?"

"We need you to *tame* them, Mister Watson."

"I don't change zombies, either," Ron said, not really sure what the fuck they were talking about. How does one tame a zombie? Whip it with a zombie rope until it jumps through a zombie hoop? Domesticate it until you can put a collar and a leash on it and take it for a walk around the block, stopping to sniff the buttholes of all the other zombies who were on leashes?

Tweedle Dipshit, or whatever the fuck his name was, spoke next. They were taking turns talking, which Ron found kind of amusing. Good cop, bad cop. "You're the biggest zombie celebrity around; you can help stop this."

"Stop what?"

The other Tweedle: "The rise of the zombies. The death. The destruction. The bro-country music."

Ron: "You're the fucking authorities and you've done this before, you stop it. Wait, did you say bro-country music?"

The first Tweedle: "Yes, Mister Watson, bro-country music. And we can't stop it."

Ron: "Why the fuck not? And what the fuck does this have to do with bro-country music? Is this about that song?"

The second Tweedle: "Yes, that song is doing something to the zombies, but we don't know what. And we can't stop it, because we don't have the antidote. You do."

Ron: "What?"

The first Tweedle: "The antidote. You have it."

Ron: "HAHAHAHAHAHAHAHAHAHAHAHAHA!" Ron fell out of his chair as he laughed; this was the funniest thing he'd heard as a zombie. Antidote? That was merely a rumor. A fantasy. There was no antidote. There was a time when he believed in such a thing, but he knew better now. He picked himself up off the ground, gathered his metal/plastic barstool, and sat down again. "There is no antidote."

The left Tweedle opened his mouth; a sigh and then some words came out. "Your daughter would disagree with you."

"Stella?"

"We didn't catch her name," the second Tweedle replied, writing in a notebook. Fuck.

"What does she know about an antidote, asshats?"

Charlie danced by and stopped. "Ron, you doing alright? You want me to get rid of these two old-timey gangsters? I can call security for you."

Ron thought about it for a moment; he knew he wasn't going to help these douchecanoes, but at the same time an antidote would be a nice thing to know about, if such a thing truly existed. Possible resurrection versus eating these two cocknuggets for a snack? It was a tough decision for a tough world.

"Nah, Charlie, they're with me," Ron replied. "We will have another round, though."

"You got it, brother. One Manhattan and two cans of piss coming up!" Bottles and cans of Coors Light started flying in the air above Charlie.

Ron stared straight ahead so he could speak to both of these motherfuckers – Tweedle Dee and Tweedle Dum – at the same time and appear to be a badass who had zero fucks to give. When, really, he was concerned. First of all, these two fucktards knew he had a daughter and now her name, and second of all, antidote? What the fuck?

"What does she know about an antidote?" Ron repeated the question while Charlie made drinks in front of him.

The twat to his left lowered his glasses and looked around Carnaval Court like he was planning a heist. Or about to reveal a secret. He leaned over to Ron and whispered the next sentence in his ear. "She makes it."

Ron laughed. Surely this douchenuggestasshatclown was mistaken, right? Stella made the antidote that might save Ron's life? What the fuck?

The drinks appeared in front of Ron and the two knuckle draggers sitting with him and Charlie walked away to help somebody else.

"You're full of shit," he replied, hoping that he was right. Or wrong. He wasn't sure at the moment.

They're full of shit, his conscience said. It was one of the rare moments he and his conscience agreed on something.

"Mister Watson," the douchelord on his right said, slowly, "Stella makes the antidote and we want it."

Ron rubbed his face, pulling off a piece of skin, and signaled for Charlie. "You're out of your fucking mind. If my daughter makes the antidote why am I still a fucking zombie?" He held up the piece of skin and showed it to Fuckface and Asstard.

Charlie danced over, with all the grace and style of a 4th grader at a mandatory school dance.

"Charlie, you can get rid of these two Rumplefuckskins now."

Instantaneously two security guards appeared on either side of the twatwaffles. "Mister Watson," Tweedle Douchedick said, as a security guard grabbed his arm, "we have Jim."

Ron turned to look at the shitstain who spoke, just as the security guard was leading him and his buddy away. "No you don't. Jim's at a stripclub right now."

The other jizztissue spoke, his voice louder as he was being led out of Carnaval Court. "We have Jim, Mister Watson, and until we get the antidote you won't see him again!"

Ron turned to his Manhattan, took a drink, and pulled out his cell phone. This couldn't be true, right? His daughter didn't make antidote and Jim *was* at a strip club right now. He was at The Booby Prize. It was his favorite, because they had a lunch buffet. And a great slogan: "The only lettuce you'll see at The Booby Prize is at the lunch buffet." He even had a girl he liked there: Mrs. Jones. Of course that wasn't her real name, but when she was called to the stage they called for 'Mrs. Jones,' and played the Billy Paul song

"Me and Mrs. Jones" over the club sound system. And Jim, who dreamed that the 'Me' in "Me and Mrs. Jones" was about him, threw money at her like a lobbyist throws money at a Congressman.

And that's where he was right now, right?

Right?

CHAPTER
16

Ron – Engaged zombie with a hall pass.
Maria – Mombie.
Stella – Young Woman.
Jim – Kidnapped and not lovin' it very much, thanks for asking.
Ron Junior – Toddler.

In a town like Las Vegas, there aren't many places to literally hide. Sure, you can hide in public, in daylight, like Ron did when he was using football field chalk to cover his decaying face, but to literally hide? So people literally don't see you, as opposed to just looking past you like they do when you hide in plain daylight? Vegas is a busy city. People all over the place. Casinos, hotels, mortuaries, all filled with people…nope, literally no place to literally hide.

Except that's not true. While classy Vegas institutions like casinos and strip clubs are full of people, there is a place in Vegas that has so very few people in it that a hostage can just hang out without being noticed. A place that people just look past, like it's hiding in plain daylight. A place that is deserted all hours of the day. A place that nobody's ever been to, but they've heard of it in scary stories told by their grandparents and *their* grandparents. A place that is the Loch Ness Monster of places. The Bigfoot of places. The compassionate politician of places.

And that place? The Vegas Valley View Public Library.

Stella picked Ron up in her newly painted matte black El Camino and they followed the KILLZ fuckers, who were driving a Nissan Cube, which, Ron thought, might be the ugliest car ever made. In fact, Ron thought, a Nissan Cube might be the baby that would be made after a WalMart fucked a Dollar Store onboard a cruise ship.

The Cube pulled into the parking lot of the Vegas Valley View Public Library and parked. The two KILLZ fuckers got out and strolled into the library like they were there to return a library book. Or look at porn on the library computers. Stella and Ron sat in the running El Camino for a second, both thinking the same thing. *Really? They have Jim in a library? This might be the first time he's ever been to a library!*

Stella pulled the El Camino into the spot next to the Cube and turned the car off. She smiled at Ron and said, "Sorry, dad."

"For what? For making the antidote? No need to be sorry, unless you're sorry you didn't give it to me already."

"I'm sorry for getting Jim kidnapped."

"You were trying to do the right thing, honey. You were trying to save the zombies. That's the most important thing, the right thing, except for giving me the antidote already." Ron glared at his daughter and paused. In his zombie-addled brain, he knew this was no time to be petty. Ron reached across the new leather bench seat of the El Camino – courtesy of the guys at the celebrity ward at Vegas Valley View Medical Center – and hugged Stella tight. "Actually honey, I'm very proud of you. And if we get out of this alive -"

"But you're already dead."

Ron glared at his daughter. "That again? The point, Stella, is that I love you very much."

"Despite the fact that I didn't give you the antidote first?"

"Yes, despite that, I love you very much. I want to tell you that in case shit gets ugly in the library." Ron laughed. "That might be the first time in the history of the world anybody's ever said 'in case shit gets ugly in the library.'"

Stella giggled and the dimples on her face giggled with her. She reminded Ron of her four-year-old self. At that age, Ron could make her dimples giggle with just a belly tickle or a fart. He felt a tear well up in his eye.

"Don't get sappy on me now, Dad," Stella said, a bit of moisture in her own eye. "Let's get Jim out of the library, where he's probably terrified because he's in a fucking library, and then I can give you some antidote and you can experience some real fucking emotions for once."

"I told you I love yo- wait, you will have more antidote after this?"

"Dad, I'm a Watson. You think I didn't save some for later?" Stella grabbed her flask of whiskey from her driver's side door. "Speaking of saving some for later, you want a swig?"

"Hell yeah, honey. Liquid courage." Ron took the flask, which was emblazoned with a picture of his face, and took a little swig of the whiskey inside. It warmed his chest and he knew that shit wouldn't get ugly in the library. It was a *library*; how ugly could shit get in it? And looking at his own face on a flask of whiskey was a little off-putting, but he was glad he chose this line of marketing versus subjecting his family to a reality TV show featuring them. Seeing his own face on a flask of whiskey was not nearly as off-putting as it would be seeing his family become the new Kardashians. As much as the money would probably be fantastic, he was pretty sure that at some point he would get tired of having cameras in his face 24 hours a day and decide that somebody filming him 24 hours a day was a good enough reason to dine on whoever was filming him 24 hours a day, and then there might be a few questions. 'Hey, what happened to the camera man?' as an example.

"Oh, and Jim already got some antidote. He's probably human right now." Stella opened the driver's side door of the El Camino and climbed out. "FYI."

"What the fuck," Ron replied. Why the fuck was he the last one to know about this? Why the fuck did he not already get antidote? Why the fuck was he not already human?

"Sorry, dad. I would have given you some, but I really wanted to be sure it worked. And when I knew it worked, you were at the bar and I didn't want to bother you."

"You can bother me for antidote, honey," Ron said, his heart proud of his beautiful daughter but his mind reeling from the thought that he could be human already. When this is over, assuming shit doesn't get ugly in the library...

And of course, shit *did* get ugly in the library. They entered through the automatic sliding doors, passing by the lone librarian in the place, who put her finger to her mouth, creating the universal symbol for *Shut the fuck up – you're in a library, asshole*, even though Ron could see that there was nobody else to offend in the library, outside of the librarian...and Jim. And the KILLZ guys, who had duct taped Jim to a chair in the historical fiction section of the library with Ron Zombie duct tape. Jim's mouth was duct taped shut with the same Ron Zombie duct tape and he wriggled uselessly against his bonds, his human arms and legs powerless against the strength of the gray tape that was originally named after a mallard. Ron knew this because, well, he was a guy, and every guy knew that 'duct tape' was originally called 'duck tape.' Duh.

"Historical fiction, huh?" Ron said as he and Stella looked around. There were more interesting parts of the library, he knew, but they must have figured nobody would be going into the historical fiction section anytime soon.

"Good choice, assholes," Stella said. "What the fuck is historical fiction, anyway? If it's history, it's not fiction!"

"Did you bring the antidote?" Tweedle Dum #1 asked.

"That'd be like creating a genre called Fictional Memoir!"

"Or Living Zombie," Ron chimed in.

"Did you bring the antidote?"

"Let him go and I'll give it to you," Stella said. She patted her backpack. "It's in here."

Jim squirmed in his chair and said something that sounded like "Mdamcl adsfjclk mmklewmew..."

Tweedle Dum pulled a semi-automatic gun out of the stacks of historical fiction, which is section 808.838 of the Dewey Decimal System, in case you were wondering, and placed the barrel against Jim's neck. And pulled the trigger.

"WHAT THE FUCK," Stella yelled in the empty library as blood squirted out of Jim's neck onto copies of *"Song of the Jay-hawk,"* a historical fiction novel that sat in the stacks next to Jim's chair. "YOU SHOT HIM!"

"So I did," Fuckface #1 said – Ron had decided he would be called Fuckface from here on out, based on what he just did. "So. I. Did. Whatcha gonna do about it?"

What the fuck, Ron thought. What are we gonna do about it? Wait, you shot him, fuckface!

"KSLK jkadsflkjl;j...." Jim said, obviously putting his two cents into the conversation. His duct-taped, bloody two cents. Ron thought about taking the duct tape off of his mouth so he could offer his suggestions in a legible manner, but he was interrupted.

"Dad you HAVE to fucking bite him!" Stella's face was a mix-ture of shock, urgency, and straight up beseechment. Ron thought she'd make a good politician with a face like that; she could express shock at how quickly jobs are leaving our country and, at the exact same time, implore people to vote for her.

"What?"

"Jeez, Dad, you have to save him! You have to bite him!"

Oh, fuck, Ron thought as blood continued to spurt from Jim's neck like it was a blood sprinkler, she's right. I have to bite him.

And there's no fucking way I'm letting my daughter be a politician. Politicians make pimps look like saints in comparison.

"Oh, fuck, Stella, you're right!"

"Of course I'm right, fuckface!"

"I'm not fuckface, honey, those guys are fuck-"

"Whatever, dad, just bite him!" Ron looked at the real fuckface #1, who was just standing there smiling, pointing his gun at Stella. When this was over, Ron thought, that guy would taste real good in a stew, with some braised ligaments and roasted tendons and potatoes. His stomach growled.

"DAD!" Stella yelled. "Are you thinking about human stew with braised ligaments and roasted tendons and potatoes again?" Damn, Ron thought, she really knows me.

"OKAY! Here I go." Ron closed his eyes and, for a minute, had some trepidation. Biting people typically made Ron hungry, and when he was hungry, he liked to eat. And when he liked to eat, people died. And when people died, well...they died. And Ron didn't really wake up today thinking he wanted to eat his best friend. He wasn't *that* hungry. Yet. Of course, if the end of the world came about and Ron and Jim were the only two humans or zombies or some combination of the above left on the planet, he'd have no trouble eating Ji -

"DAD! Are you thinking about the end of the world again and having to eat Jim again?"

"OKAY!" Suddenly Ron remembered that he'd done this before, when Jim got shot while rescuing Ron, so he took a deep breath and relaxed. It was going to be more comfortable than the first time, like making love to your new girlfriend the second ti – *no, no it wasn't, bitch. Biting Jim is not like making love to a woman the second time. It's like biting Jim, fuckface.* This time Ron welcomed his conscience's interruption and smiled. Then he leaned down, pulled Jim's shirt up, and bit Jim on the chest, near the mark he left last time he bit Jim on the chest. Jim tasted delicious, of course, because Ron was hungry, but Ron's conscience took over to distract him from the fact that his best friend tasted good. *The Big Red Machine is the nickname given to the Cincinnati Reds baseball team which dominated the National League from 1970 to 1976. The team is widely recognized as being among the best teams in baseball history. Over that span, the team won five National League West Division titles, four National League pennants, and two World Series titles. The team's combined record from 1970-1976 was 683 wins and 443 losses, an average of nearly 98 wins per season. Bitch.*

Ron snapped out of his distraction and looked down as Jim stirred. Ron put his hand on Jim's forehead; "Jim, buddy, everything's gonna be okay."

"Dad, don't lie to him." Stella clearly disagreed. "He's a zombie again."

"Well, yeah," Ron said, as Jim, still tied to his chair, stirred again. "There's that." He put his mouth next to Jim's ear and whispered. "Everything's gonna be okay…except you're a zombie again."

"RAWWWWWWWWWWWWR" Jim's eyes shot open like he just got hit in the testicles with a major league line drive and Stella screamed. Jim looked around, saw her, burst through the flimsy duct tape holding him to the chair and went after Stella like trailer park dwellers at WalMart going after the latest video game console on Black Friday. Ron tackled him before he could get to her.

"No, Jim," Ron yelled, "Stella is friends, not food!"

"RAWWWWWWWWR!" Jim said, a less articulate sentence than Ron had been used to him using. To Ron, who was on top of Jim, Jim seemed…different. Less evolved than he was a few minutes ago.

"He's a fucking zombie, dad! He went back to the beginning!"

Holy fuck, Ron thought, she's right. He didn't pick up where he left off as a highly evolved, intelligent, wisecracking zombie; he went back to being a zombie who wanted nothing but BRAINS.

Fuckface #2 laughed and spoke. "Now give him the antidote."

Stella looked up at him. "What?"

"The antidote. Give it to him."

"Fuck you!"

"Stella!"

"Um, sorry, *sir*, Antidote? I don't know what you're talking about."

Fuckface #1 took his semi-automatic gun and placed it against Ron's head. "Give him the antidote or I shoot your father. In the head. And, as we all know" he looked at Fuckface #2, who laughed, "no antidote can help that."

Stella looked at Ron, who was still sitting on Jim, who was trying to get up to go eat Stella, who was looking at Ron, who was *still* sitting on Jim.

"And if I shoot your father in the head," Fuckface #1 said, "There'll be a fresh zombie loose in this room. And only we," He looked at #2 and smiled, "have the key to the door."

Stella smirked; "If I give him the antidote, fuckface, even if I even have the antidote to give him, let's say, what happens after that? I've seen enough movies and cop shows to know you're not going to just let us go. What's to keep you from killing us? Oh, and by the way, the doors are fucking automatic. Shitforbrains."

"We just want to know if the antidote works, that's all," #1 said with a grin on his face. "Orders."

"Orders," #2 repeated.

"Of course," Ron said, from atop Jim, with a gun still to his head. "Orders. Just doing your job. That's all you guys know."

"HEY," #2 said, "DO YOU HAVE A FUCKING JOB, ASSHOLE?"

"Wow," Ron said, "sensitive much?"

"WELL, DO YOU?"

"For your information, I do not. Yet."

"THEN YOU WOULDN'T UNDERSTAND A FUCKING GOOD WORK ETHIC, WOULD YOU?"

The gun pressed a little bit harder into Ron's skull and he decided it might be in his best interests to play along, despite the ridiculousness of the situation. "No, you're right. I'm a bum who wouldn't know how to do a job if I had one." He winked at Stella.

"THAT'S RIGHT. NOW YOU," Fuckface #2 pointed at Stella with his gun, "GIVE HIM THE FUCKING ANTIDOTE."

"Please stop yelling," Stella said, "You're annoying." She reached down the front of her shirt and pulled up her necklace, which had a vial on it. "The antidote is right here."

"RAWWWWWWWWR!"

"Hurry, honey," Ron said, as he sat on Jim who was wiggling around like he was jello wrestling, "I can't hold him down much longer."

Stella opened the antidote vial, smelled it, and said, "Yep, still fresh."

"It goes bad?" #2 asked.

"Have you ever mixed Nutella with yak blood? It's nasty after a couple of days. Smells like your mom's vagina."

#1 laughed and pointed at #2. "Haha! She's been with your mom!"

#2 pressed his gun further into Ron's skull. If he had pushed any harder, the gun would have been in China. "Fuck you! My mom's vagina smells like fucking roses!"

Ron, Stella, #1, and even Jim paused. As they all looked around sheepishly, the awkwardness in the room was as heavy as a military tank.

#2 finally broke the ice. "Fuck you! Give him the motherfucking antidote!"

"Orders?" Stella said.

"ORDERS," #2 yelled.

"Okay, one Your Mom's Rosy Vagina coming up!"

Flippy strolled through the automatic doors to the library, his face alight with a smile as he looked around. "You rang? And wow, what the fuck is this place? I've heard of libraries, but I didn't know Vegas had one!" He walked over to Stella as #1 and #2 pointed their automatic weapons at his bald head.

"Who's this guy?" #2 yelled.

Stella handed the vial of the antidote to Flippy. "It's part of the process, fuckface. Flippy has to give it to him or it doesn't work."

"Seriously?" Ron asked.

"Seriously," Stella replied.

"So wait, all this time -" Ron started.

"Hold him tight, Dad!"

Flippy took the vial and walked over to Jim, who was still being held down by Ron's bodyweight. He looked like Ron's comfortable zombie couch.

Ron opened Jim's mouth with his good hand as Flippy approached with the vial of antidote. He held it over Jim's mouth and poured like he was pouring free shots at Carnaval Court.

"Who the fuck are you? What the fuck are you doing?" Jim asked. "Ron, get off of me! Who are these fuckers?"

"Wow, that was fast," Ron said as he slowly stood up. He didn't want to take any chances; he had seen enough horror movies to know that nothing was ever as it seemed and that things that appeared to be safe would often be the things that killed you. So, as he stood up, he assumed his kung-fu pose, directed at Jim. With only one good arm. He looked like a paper crane, ripped in half.

"What the hell is wrong with everybody," Jim asked as he got up and dusted himself off. "And where the fuck are we? Is this a *library*? Why the fuck are we at a library?"

"He's picking up where he left off," #1 said. "Very interesting." Then he pulled his semi-automatic gun out of section 808.838 of the library again and shot Jim in the neck. Again.

"WHAT THE FUCK," Stella demanded.

"We have to make sure," #2 said, with a smile. "Bite him and give him the antidote again."

"Make sure what?" Ron asked. "Make sure you're both assholes?"

"We have to make sure the antidote works," #1 said. "Orders."

"Fuck you and your orders," Ron said.

"Bite him or he dies," #1 said, pointing to Jim, who was spilling more blood from his new wound and adding to the blood that was already on the floor of section 808.838 of the Vegas Valley View Library. It was like a blood library. A blood bank, Ron thought. Blood begets blood. Kinda like the gun control policies of this country.

"Oh, fuck, alright," Ron said, as he leaned over, lifted Jim's shirt up, and bit him on the chest. Again. Next to the last mark he left on Jim's chest last time. And again, Jim was delicious.

But before Ron's conscience could start filling him in on the spectacular sports qualities of the 1970s Pittsburgh Steelers, aka "The Steel Curtain," Flippy showed up and was pouring antidote down Jim's throat like...well, like he was pouring free shots at the bar at Carnaval Court.

And again Jim revived. "RAWWW...hey, what the fuck? Why am I laying on the floor in the library again? This place gives me the heebie-jeebies."

And #1 shot Jim again.

And Ron bit Jim again.

And Flippy gave Jim the antidote again.

And so on. And so on. And so on.

It was like "Who's On First," zombie style. Like Laurel and Hardy had a baby that turned out to be Satan. Like Lucifer had possessed all the members of Monty Python.

Until finally, Motherfucker #1 was satisfied that the antidote works. "Okay, I'm satisfied that the antidote works."

"Finally! Fuck, I'm exhausted," Jim said. "Living and dying and living and dying is tiring."

"I'm exhausted, too!" Flippy said, as he looked at his watch, his bald head shining under the shitty overhead fluorescent lights of the library. "Can I go back to work now?"

"Yeah, can we all go now?" Ron asked, as he mentally prepared a stew that these two douchebags would be part of tonight at dinner.

"You can go, but you must leave the antidote. And Flippy."

"No fucking way," Stella said. #2 pointed his gun at Ron's head. "Oh, you mean this antidote?" She pointed to the vial on the necklace out in front of her Chrissie Hynde t-shirt. "Sure, you can have it. And this Flippy?" She motioned to Flippy, who shrugged and went to stand by #2. Stella took the vial from her neck and held it tight. "If I give this to you how do we know you're not going to kill us anyway?"

"You'll just have to trust me," #2 said, laughing the way your friends laugh when they invite you to a 'little gathering with some friends' that is, in real life, an orgy at your ex-girlfriend's house. Stella quickly caught on to the deceit, wound up like Nolan Ryan on a good day, and flung the vial containing the antidote across the library stacks towards the computer area, where a homeless man sat, looking at porn. The vial bounced off of the industrial strength library carpet and skidded under the homeless man's chair, where it co-mingled with all of the homeless man's belongings. Meaning a bottle of whiskey and a Pee-Chee folder where the homeless man was keeping notes on all of his favorite types of pornography.

"You better go get it, fuckers, because the antidote self-destructs after 30 seconds when in contact with pornography."

#1's eyes opened wide and he took off running towards the homeless man; #2 hesitated for a second, shot Jim in the neck again, and followed along. Orders, right?

"Bite him again and let's go," Stella said.

Ron bit Jim again, quickly, without even thinking about it, like a guy who cleans outhouses for a living and has just finished his first month on the job. Rote. "Does the antidote really self de-struct?" Ron asked. His daughter was very, very smart; a porno self-destruct mechanism was not out of her realm of invention.

"Really, dad?"

On second thought, Ron thought, maybe a porno self-destruct mechanism was outside of her realm of invention...

"Let's go, before those morons get back."

Ron, Stella, and Jim grabbed Flippy's hand and the motley foursome ran through the historical fiction section, the circula-tions section, periodicals (where Ron noticed a new magazine called "Werewolf Life" which was, ironically, right next to "Hipster Life") and the non-historical fiction section before reaching the front door of the library. Ron turned and looked behind them; in the distance he could see that the two KILLZ guys – Tweedle Dee and Tweedle Dum – or Fuckface #1 and Fuckface #2 – were beat-ing the shit out of the homeless man. Resisting the urge to start making that stew he dreamed up, he joined Stella, Flippy and Jim, and all four of them went through the automatic library doors into the hot Vegas sun.

CHAPTER
17

Ron – Zombie.
Maria – Mombie.
Stella – Young Woman.
Jim – Zombie and over it.
Ron Junior – Toddler.

Have you ever wanted to be a better version of yourself? Visually or spiritually or otherwise? Like maybe you'd like to be 20 pounds lighter or have different color hair or be exceedingly wealthy or spend all your time working with children in third world countries? In this modern world, it's not such a crazy notion, is it? Look at butt implants; the only reason a butt implant is performed is because the implantee is looking for a better version of themselves. Same with face lifts or a college education or buying a new sports car.

Or becoming human. Ron had decided long ago that all he really wanted to be was human again; to be a better version of his zombie self. Well, okay, sometimes his desire for fame got in the way of his desire to be a human, but everybody's allowed a fuck up once in awhile, right? That's what makes us human. Ironically.

And here was his chance to be human. Stella had given the KILLZ Order Guys her antidote, but of course she had more of the antidote in the glove box of her El Camino. It was antidote mix, actually, so it wasn't really antidote and was missing an ingredient, but it was only missing one ingredient: Nutella. Some students at VVVJC were allergic to hazelnuts, so Stella tried to keep Nutella out of the chemistry lab as much as possible.

Stella and Maria stayed behind at the apartment one night to look after Ron Junior while Ron and Jim went out to find some Nutella, the final ingredient they needed to become human again. Why the fuck it was required for the antidote, Ron didn't know, but his daughter was smarter than he, was so he didn't ask. He just went to find some. It couldn't be that difficult, could it? Nutella is simply a delicious hazelnut spread and had to be available everywhere.

Of course that's not true. Jim and Ron set out in the El Camino, Jim driving, down one of Vegas' never ending ribbons of asphalt and, after about five minutes, they looked at each other and asked, simultaneously, "Where the fuck are we going?" Ron rolled his eyes, pondered for a minute, and asked, satirically, "The Nutella store?"

"They have those?" Jim asked, his eyebrows high on his face. "Like the Apple Store, but with delicious hazelnut spread instead of nerds?"

"Shit, I don't know," Ron said. "Would a Nutella store have a genius bar? Like you walk in with a broken jar of Nutella and they fix it for you or suggest you upgrade your Nutella system? Or get the new Nutella tablet?"

"Hahahaha!" Jim laughed heartily, a zombie on the verge of becoming human again. It was all so surreal, but the jokes helped. Humor always helps the tension in serious situations, Ron thought.

"Why don't we just go to the grocery store?"

Jim looked at Ron and smiled. "You're a fucking genius, you know that?"

"Fuck yes I do," Ron said, and sat back on his leather covered 1968 El Camino bench seat, putting his head on the headrest. Ah, the feel of a leather seat. Thank you, celebrity maternity ward! Sure, his celebrity might have been fleeting, but he sure enjoyed it while it was fleeting. And now? Now he was about to leave that permanently behind and become permanently human. Permanently. It was such a permanent word.

Jim pulled the El Camino into a Vons parking lot; one of 83 Vons parking lots in Las Vegas. America had long ago given up on offering its citizens much grocery shopping choice outside of Vons, Safeway, WalMart, and the like. Good thing it was convenient and conveniently laid out; you've been in one Vons, you've been in them all.

They shambled into the Vons, a zombie and his recently hostaged zombie friend, two dark characters in search of that which would make them light: Nutella.

"Hi, welcome to Vons," the lithe blonde night clerk, 'Sandra' by her name tag, said cheerfully. Damn, Ron thought, Sandra Nightclerk (her name, in his mind) has a nice ass. Too bad I'm engaged to be married.

"Cheerio," Jim said with a faux British accent, "Can you kindly direct us to the Nutella, young lass? We are but travelers from a distant place, as you can tell, trying to get home. The Queen awaits!"

"You're British!" Sandra Nightclerk said with glee. "I love British people! Can I take a picture with you?"

Ron smiled and said, with his best British accent, which he picked up listening to Keith Richards speak on Rolling Stones bootlegs, "That would be fab!"

Sandra Nightclerk grabbed her phone, put it on a selfie stick, stood next to Ron and Jim, and snapped a picture in front of a towering display of Nutella, conveniently located in front of the store, right by the cash registers. And that's when all hell broke loose.

"ALL RIGHT YOU MOTHERFUCKERS, EVERYBODY DOWN ON THE GROUND."

Ron turned towards the entrance of the Vons and saw a pair of dark figures, not unlike he and Jim....except these dark figures were wearing masks over their heads and pointing high powered rifles at Sandra Nightclerk. And everybody else. Often all at once.

"EVERYBODY DOWN!"

Ron sighed. Here he was, trying to secure some Nutella, trying to get back his light, his life, via Nutella, which was right behind him, stacked to the ceiling, and some fucking asshole with a narcissistic bent and a giant rifle was trying to get in his way. Granted, this fucking asshole didn't realize who he was dealing with, but still – Ron needed the Nutella. He needed life. So he got down on the ground.

As he lay on the ground next to Jim, Sandra Nightclerk laid down between them and spoke in a whisper. "You're British, do something!"

Ron pondered this; were the British known for doing something in a robbery? Maybe something James Bond-ish? Sure, he could probably find a way to turn the Nutella display into sharks with laser beams on their heads....

"DON'T FUCKING TALK! DON'T FUCKING MOVE!"

"Um, I hate to tell you this," Ron said to Sandra Nightclerk, laying next to him on the ground, "but we're not British."

"Then what is that accent?"

Oh, shit, Ron realized, he was still channeling Keith Richards who, honestly, could have been a zombie for the last 40 years and nobody would have been surprised. Has there ever been more of a walking corpse than Keith Richards?

"Oh, sorry, love."

"Still with the accent."

"Shit," Ron said, without an accent, finally. "Sorry."

Ron's right temple felt cold and realized that while he was wasting time being Keith Richards or Ringo Starr or whoever, one of the two masked men had stealthily walked over and was now holding a gun to his head.

"I SAID DON'T FUCKING TALK!"

Ron looked up. "Sorry."

"DON'T FUCKING TALK!"

Ron said 'sorry' again, but this time with his eyes. He looked a lot like a puppy dog who didn't know where that pee on the carpet came from, thank you very much.

"YOU, GET UP." The masked man was yelling at Sandra Night-clerk, who was still laying between Ron and Jim. She quickly got to her feet and the masked man put his gun against her temple. The other masked man came over to her other side, so there was one masked man standing in front of Ron and one standing in front of Jim.

"YOU'RE GOING TO SHOW US TO THE SAFE, BITCH. NOW."

Sandra Nightclerk started crying and the first masked man slapped her. "NOW!"

Oh, no, Ron thought, all I am here for is Nutella, but you just hit a woman. YOU HIT A WOMAN. This was all of a sudden about waaaaaaay more than Nutella and life. And somebody smelled like fried chicken. And Ron LOVED fried chicken. His stomach growled.

Ron looked over at Jim, now that he could see him again, and they communicated with their eyes, as only two best friends could. After a minute of silent mental telepathic planning, they each reached up and took a bite out of the Achilles Heel of the masked man standing in front of each of them.

"MOTHERFUUUUUUUUUUU" the two masked men yelped in unison as they fell to the ground, their weapons skidding harmlessly across the linoleum Vons floor and landing safely below a giant Pokemon Go display. Ron realized the sound could have been an Olympic sport: Synchronized Cursing.

Synchronized Eating could also have been an Olympic sport, and Ron and Jim would have excelled at it. As they begin to dine on these masked morons who tried to hold up a Vons in Vegas,

Ron looked up at Sandra Nightclerk, and said, "You might want to look away. This could get ugly."

"Or delicious," Jim said, blood running down his chin as his masked man writhed in agony from the hole in his chest. Damn, Ron thought, you work fast.

"Maria asked me to become a vegetarian, but today is my cheat day." Ron looked down at his sweat pants. "Good thing I wore my buffet pants. And damn, you work fast, Jim."

"I really wanted my babyback babyback babyback ribs...."

"It was," Ron couldn't resist as he bit into his moron's breast, "the breast of times, it was the worst of times."

"I'm really glad this party had," Jim replied, as he nibbled on his moron's hand, "finger foods."

"Liver let die," Ron said, as he went after his moron's yes, liver. Duh.

As it was presumably their last meal as zombies, Ron and Jim both reveled in the ceremony of the event. Calling it their "Last Supper," they took their time tasting each and every muscle and ligament of the two men who tried to rob the store. They sorted the bones of the bodies after they were finished and created their own Nutella display, a tower of bones featuring Nutella. Sandra Nightclerk took pictures of both of them posing in front of the tower and posted the pictures on her "British People of Vons" social media site as Ron and Jim high-fived each other. Then they took turns turkey bowling, since it was November. The night clerk set up ten 2-liter bottles of orange soda in the frozen foods aisle while Ron and Jim took turns sliding frozen turkeys down that linoleum floor, knocking down as many bottles of orange soda as they could, using the freezers on both sides of the aisle as bumpers, speaking in British accents the whole time. It was the best night of the night clerk's life, as she documented on her social media site. "British People Of Vons Go Turkey Bowling" got more likes than any post since "Bad British Teeth of Vons," back in 2014.

Ron and Jim left Sandra Nightclerk and the bloody, slippery, frozen-turkey infested Vons after an hour, two friends who were celebrating their last night as zombies, their 'Last Supper,' and went home to find their way home....to humanhood. Via a delicious hazelnut cocoa spread.

CHAPTER
18

Ron – Zombie.
Maria – Zombie.
Stella – Young Adult.
Jim – Zombie.
Ron Junior – Toddler.

Humans gather together for all kinds of reasons. To celebrate, to mourn, to watch sports, to commit crimes…something about the communal experience of being in a group of people, participating in the same thing as everybody else, feeling like you're the best group of people in the whole wide fucking world, enhances the human experience dramatically.

And then sometimes you just get together to take drugs. Ron knew nothing about that. NOTHING.

Back at Ron and Maria's apartment, Ron, Maria and Jim gathered around the Nutella. Ron had grabbed ten jars of it, just in case whatever, and they were all arranged in a pentagram shape on the circular Formica dining table in the kitchen. Nobody was really into devil worship or Aleister Crowley or the occult or whatever, but they all agreed that if these magical jars of Nutella were going to be arranged in a shape, it should be a pentagram. Something about this whole idea that Nutella (and whatever Stella was going to add to it) could turn them back into humans was very occult-ish.

"So, honey, all we gotta do is eat Nutella?" Maria asked, a sarcastic smile on her face. She was wearing black yoga pants and a sports bra, as Stella told her to wear clothes she could move around in. Yoga pants were Ron's favorite pants for women – he thought whoever invented them should be awarded a Nobel Peace Prize – and yoga pants on Maria were his favorite thing in the whole world, clothes-wise, because they showed off her amazing heart-shaped ass.

"Well, duh," Ron said, returning the sarcastic smile. "Nutella is a delicious hazelnut spread. Everybody should eat it." He was wearing jorts – jean shorts – because he had no fashion sense and because they were comfortable, and a 'Ron Zombie' t-shirt. He had a whole box full of those fucking things.

"Everybody except the allergic fucks," Jim said, a smile on his face, workout pants and a moisture-wicking shirt adorning his fit zombie body. Fit because when he ate, he avoided the fatty areas of his victim's bodies. And because when he was a lifeguard in high school, he learned how to take care of his body. Principles that applied even when he was a zombie…which he hopefully wouldn't be for much longer.

Stella was in the kitchen, standing over a boiling pot of something that smelled so awful, even Ron Junior noticed. "WAAAAAAAAAAAAAH" he protested as the putrid scent wafted into every room of the tiny apartment.

"I know, brother," Stella said, as he rocked in his automatic rocking bassinet emblazoned with his daddy's picture on the side above the words 'Rockin' Zombie.' "It smells like poop but will taste like shit. Good thing *you* don't have to eat it."

"WAAAAAAAAH!"

Stella turned off the burner and stirred the strange concoction in front of her. "We're almost out of yak blood, so it's good we're doing this now," she said. "And there's a sentence I never thought I'd say."

Ron looked over at his genius daughter and smiled. As much as things were fucked up all over, he was very confident in the fact that she was going to be the one to save the world...and it would start right here, right now.

"You guys ready?"

Ron looked at Jim, who looked at Maria, who looked at Ron. And vice versa. And so on. Then all three of them giggled stupidly, like they were a bunch of teenage boys about to see somebody's hot mom naked. It was a moment that they all knew they probably would never forget, even if it didn't work. Because even if it didn't work, imagine the stories! "Remember that time we thought we could be human? Hahahahaha! Boy, were we gullible!" And if it did work...Ron didn't really want to think about that. He had dreamed of it so many times, and so many times it didn't happen, so many times it didn't even have a chance of happening, that he felt like if he dreamed of it one more time and it didn't happen again he might go crazy. As crazy as a zombie can go, anyway.

"Yeah, we're ready," Jim said. All three of them sat down at the circular table, with the jars of Nutella in front of them, and Maria grabbed Ron's hand under the table. Then Jim grabbed Ron's other hand. "I'm scared," he whispered loud enough for everybody to hear.

"Don't be scared, man," Ron said, putting on his best 'camp counselor' voice. He too, was scared, but camp counselors never let the campers know that. "We have nothing to lose; we're already zombies. And we already drink things that taste like shit – Lite Beer, anybody? – so think of this as just a Tuesday at the bar!"

"Then where's Rob? And Charlie? And everybody else?"

"Okay, fucker. I was trying to help."

The door to the apartment opened and Flippy burst through, in his signature black 'Carnaval Court' shirt, shorts, running shoes, bald head, and unforced, childlike grin. "Did somebody ask for free shots at the bar?"

"Flippy!" Ron, Jim and Maria all yelled in unison, like three teenage boys actually seeing somebody's hot mom naked. Ron realized it was probably Jim's hot mom, based on the commotion, because Jim's mom was HOT. As much as Ron could remember, anyway. She looked a lot like Heather Locklear, circa 1995. And everybody knew that Heather Locklear, circa 1995, *was* HOT.

Flippy took the concoction from the stove and threw it up in the air like it was liquid cotton candy, and it landed in a giant stainless steel cup on the linoleum bar with a splash. Then, he poured the contents of that cup into a brown bottle with a label on it, a label that had the word "antidote" written on it with a marker. Almost like he was prepared for this, Ron thought. What the fuck? How was he seemingly always ready to give out antidote?

Next, Flippy climbed up on the circular Formica table with his bottle and poured a shot of Ass Juice into the cups set in front of each of the three of them. Ass Juice was what Ron called it, since it smelled like ass and resembled juice. "Now add a teaspoon full of Nutella to each cup and down it," Stella said. "Quickly."

Ron opened the jar of Nutella in front of him and took a teaspoon and scooped the Nutella onto it, as the others did the same. He held his teaspoon up. "Cheers."

"Cheers," Jim said.

"Cheers, bitches," Maria said, with a smile on her face.

"Goo-gooooo," Ron Junior said, which probably means *where's my fucking Nutella, bitches?*, but nobody really knows for sure. Shouldn't humans have invented a baby translator by now? We can go to the moon and we can change a zombie back to human but we can't translate toddler speak?

Ron stopped worrying what Ron Junior was saying, mostly because he was obviously calm and content at the moment, but also because Ron's spoon had started to drip Nutella. And everybody knows you don't waste Nutella, under any circumstances, so he stuck his spoon into the stinky ass cup in front of him and stirred.

And downed the contents of the cup as Maria and Jim did the same.

And then they sat there, three doomed souls around a Formica table in a tiny apartment on the outskirts of Las Vegas, and waited.

And waited.

And waited.

And waited.

"Um, Stella, honey," Ron said, without sounding like a fucking back seat driver, because he hated it when people did that to him, "How long is this going to take?"

Stella looked at her watch, raised her eyes, smiled sweetly at her dad, sent Flippy out the front door, and put on a hockey helmet with a full cage. Where the fuck did she get that, Ron wondered.

"Until about…" Stella looked at her watch again and pushed Ron Junior's crib into the adjacent bedroom and closed the door. "3, 2, 1….now."

Ron's legs started to twitch and he looked at Maria and Jim, who both had wide eyes like they had just been caught cheating with the nanny. What the fuck was this? Ron's head floated like a hot air balloon at a hot air balloon festival and words scrolled across the top of his mind quickly, like one of those LED scrolling light signs you might see in the window of a nail shop in the poor part of town. NUTELLA. PERSONA. TIBIA. VAGINA. BRAIN-SIA. Why did every word end in 'A'? Ron felt like he was drunk. Or high. Or on LSD. Or turning human.

Ron's feet started moving, Stella curled up into a ball, and the next thing Ron knew he was dancing around the room like Britney Spears on speed. NUTELLA. Jim and Maria were also dancing around like crazy people, their heads shaking left and right, faster and faster, like they wanted to separate from their necks. PERSONA. Their legs swinging around as if they were on their own, six wild limbs moving separately from three crazy bodies, like broken Barbie dolls. TIBIA. Stella crouched in the corner with her helmet on, a grizzled veteran of the zombie wars. VAGINA. Pictures tumbling off the walls, furniture flipped over, a minefield of Home Depot accoutrements. BRAINSIA.

And when it was over a few minutes later it looked a lot like somebody had had an all-night meth party the night before. Stuff everywhere, like an episode of 'Hoarders' had been filmed there. Stench everywhere, like several cats had died a month ago and been allowed to decompose right there in Ron and Maria's Pretty Good Room. It was a Great Room when the apartment was new, but in this post-recession zombie world, its status had fallen, like a predatory lender after a government hearing.

And, like a meth party day after, there were three bodies on the floor, passed out. Three *human* bodies.

"I think they used a bit too much Nutella," Stella said, stepping over the human bodies, and went to get Ron Junior ready for bed.

CHAPTER
19

Ron – Human.
Maria – Human.
Stella – Young Adult.
Jim – Human.
Ron Junior – Toddler.

The first time you have sex – nay, make love with somebody you truly love – it can be intimidating. Skin you've never touched before, lips you've never kissed, nude body you've never seen, erogenous zones you've never explored. You don't know how your new partner is going to feel, taste, or react to your mad skillz as a lover. If all goes well, you have a superb evening of orgasm after orgasm, every touch with your finger or tongue or genitalia or elbow or heel or selfie stick leading to pleasure for your partner and vice versa.

Sometimes, however, the newness of the situation can lead to a little, uh, apprehensiveness on your part. Particularly if you're a man. You finally get this wonderful woman, whom you've already decided you're going to marry and have babies with and grow old with and eat split pea soup with at the assisted living facility in 50 years, into bed, and the rush of her beautiful body and naked skin and passionate moans leads to trepidation on your part. Flaccid trepidation. Don't worry, it happens to the best of us. The FIRST time.

Ron didn't have this problem, at all. Not this time. As human Maria took off her pretty summer dress, the erection in his cargo shorts was as stiff as the Devil's Tower. He attributed it to the fact that it had been awhile and that he wasn't thinking about eyeballs, he wasn't thinking about tibias or fibias or sucking on some poor soul's big toe to get the meat out; no, he was thinking about her. Maria's skin was as flawless as a fresh snow, and her smile was that of the purest sunshine. Ron marveled at whatever good fortune had gotten him to this point and realized that his eyes were wet. He immediately started making excuses for it to himself – "It's raining on my face!" "I've been cutting onions!" "My eyes are sweaty!" – and realized that no, this time, his eyes were wet because he was human. And being human was all he ever wanted.

Maria stood before him, naked and human. That's really when you're most naked and human, right? Right before you're about to make love to somebody you really care about? As Maria approached him and he grabbed her hips, Ron realized this was the definition of *intimacy. Human intimacy.*

"You're a brick house," he whispered.

He kissed her neck; her skin was as soft as a silk pillow and her smell…well, she smelled like a human. Not a zombie. This was how he remembered her from the first time they met, when she was a human and he was a zombie.

Was.

"Let's get it on," she purred, her eyes heavy with desire.

"You're a super freak," he whispered, his newly human brain deliriously ablaze with sensation and want, like a reformed vegetarian about to sit down to a perfectly cooked steak dinner.

Maria reached down and undid Ron's shorts, letting them drop to the floor. His underwear looked like a pup tent. "I'm too sexy for these pants," he murmured. Maria laughed, reached down, and slowly removed the pup tent, exposing his erect penis....which was pink. Not black. *Pink*. HUMAN PINK.

"DAMN," Maria said. "You dropped a bomb on me! That is one fine piece of meat you have there, Mister Watson."

Ron giggled. His penis was pink! The antidote worked!

"Little pink corvette," he whispered.

"Baby, you're much too fast" she purred.

"Love to love you baby," he cooed.

"Shake your booty," she hummed.

"Disco inferno," he murmured.

"Burn baby burn," she softly spoke, her eyes perfectly aligned with his own, like the only two pieces of a jigsaw puzzle.

"I wanna sex you up," he replied, his desire increasing as if he were hiking Longs Peak in Colorado and was a few minutes from the summit.

"It's business time," she said, with a grin.

"I did it all for the nookie," he retorted, "come on, the nookie, come on."

"Seriously?"

"I'm kidding, you sexy thing," Ron replied, and nibbled on her ear.

Maria gasped, grabbed his penis, stroked it with her right hand, and giggled. "Just talkin' 'bout shaft!"

"Shut yo' mouth! Brains!" Ron said, his eyes rolled up in his head.

"Brains!" Maria said, and stood up, her bare vagina in front of his face. Ron eyes returned to the front of his face and he looked up and shot her a glance that said, "Get ready, I'm going in." Then he did that just that, using his tongue and lips to explore every little bit of her human womanhood, her Fuckingham Palace, Ron's favorite palace, where every stroke of his tongue – he was writing poems on her clitoris with his tongue – produced a little bit more erotic excitement in Maria until she exploded (not literally, because that would be gross and not very erotic at all), and the sky rained down a thousand stars and the earth opened up and she used up every ounce of orgasmic ability she had…and then Ron went in again, writing novels this time, and Maria came again… and then Ron went in again and Maria came AGAIN…to Ron, it was like he could do no wrong. His tongue fit perfectly in Maria's clitoris, like he had gone to Home Depot and purchased the perfect screw to put a porch swing together, which everybody knows NEVER fucking happens on the first trip to Home Depot, and every time his tongue got close to Maria's clitoris, she came. She came and she came. She came in waves, like her body was the ocean. She came in fits, like she was the driving beat behind a rock and roll song. And she came consecutively, like she was the alphabet.

And then, when she appeared to be taking a break from orgasms, Ron took his turn and summited… and it was the best seven seconds of his life.

CHAPTER
20

Ron – Human.
Maria – Human.
Stella – Young Adult.
Jim – Human.
Ron Junior – Toddler.

A wedding, in reality, is really not much more than a party for the bride and groom's friends. Sure, it is a tying of a metaphorical knot – or, in some cases, a real knot, if your life together is complicated – but really, it's a chance for the friends of the couple to have a good time. Eating, drinking, dancing to music they'd never dance to anywhere else – "YMCA," anybody? – and posing for pictures that will get stuck in a leather-bound picture book that will live on a shelf at home for however many years the couple stayed married.

Ron believed all of that. Ron also realized that the wedding choices weren't up to him, so, being the enlightened human being that he was – even though he still couldn't believe he was a *human* – he delegated all wedding decisions to his lovely bride, Maria. He loved her more than life itself – and more importantly, he trusted her more than life itself – so he left all of it in her capable hands and hoped for the best.

When she came back with, "It's really just a party for our friends," Ron knew that he had met his soul mate.

And, being that their wedding would be mostly a party for their friends, and being that many of their friends worked at Carnaval Court, and being that Carnaval Court was a bar, which meant that the guests could drink, and being that The Whipits were the Carnaval Court band, which meant that the guests could dance, Ron and Maria decided to have their wedding in New Mexico.

Just kidding.

Carnaval Court on this Tuesday – it was the only day of the week that wouldn't cost them an arm and a leg, no pun intended, to rent, because who the fuck drinks on a Tuesday? – was completely decorated for a wedding. Well, not just any wedding; it was decorated for a wedding of former zombies. Rob had wrapped the bar in black, for Ron, while Charlie had wrapped the chairs in white, for Maria. And the stage was wrapped in red, because Flippy, Vache, and The Whipits thought there should be some blood in the ceremony somehow.

And Robyn, the lone female bartender at Carnaval Court, was going to be the minister; she had recently been ordained in the Church of the Purple Unicorn – an online ministry that could ordain her quickly enough for this wedding – and was eager to officiate her first wedding. Sure, the Purple Unicorn standard vows were wacky, with all kinds of things about Purple and unicorns, duh, but Robyn had written her own non-unicorny vows and was going to try them out today.

Maria was dressed in a sweet white wedding dress that Stella had received from a friend in the Vegas wedding dress industry; it made her look like a sexy angel, Ron thought. His sexy angel. His sexy *human* angel. The realization still boggled his head. His *human* head. He was *human* and he was marrying a *human* woman today and would go on to live a *human* life, with a son and a white picket fence and a house in the suburbs and holymotherfuck, he still couldn't believe it.

Stella, the Maid of Honor, was dressed in a Debbie Harry t-shirt and black jeans but, to her credit, she was wearing makeup. Goth makeup, but still. Makeup. Getting Stella to wear any makeup was like getting Congress to act on anything.

And Ron and Jim? White velour track suits from the Mirage. Yeah, possibly not the most fashion-forward outfits they could have picked, but Ron didn't want to wear black, for the simple reason that he wasn't dead anymore. He was a *human*, so he wanted to wear white, which felt like a human color, because it was the exact opposite of black. And it was a virginesque color, and Ron felt virginesque, relatively, because he'd only had human sex with Maria once and his side of the human sex had lasted all of seven seconds. And that almost didn't count, right?

All that said, when he looked in his closet that morning to pick something out to wear – typical fucking man, waiting until the last minute, right? – the only white thing he had was the velour track suit. Well, that and his tighty-whities, but nobody wanted to see that, he was sure.

And the guests? Athena, Crystal and Sidney were there, as was Sandra Nightclerk and Doctor Roberts from Vegas Valley View Hospital, who was wearing her signed "Ron Zombie" t-shirt atop an unsigned "Ron Zombie" poodle skirt, "Ron Zombie" saddle shoes, and a "Ron Zombie" scarf in her black hair. She looked like she was the leader of the Pink Zombies, like the Pink Ladies from "Grease." Zombie Howard Cosell was there, looking even more decrepit than before. And sounding more decrepit. "This. Is. Howard. Cosell. And. I'm. Dead." Bel Biv Devoe wanted to come, but Tony used to be in the band – back then, it was Bel Biv Devoe Kouns – and that ended poorly, so there was bad blood between The Whipits and BBD. And Ron preferred The Whipits anyway, all things considered.

On the bar were scattered pictures that Ron had taken since he had become a zombie and met Maria. There were pictures of him ogling Maria's ass on the airplane the day they met, pictures of the muscle cars outside of her apartment, pictures of her in a Las Vegas Wranglers hockey jersey, pictures of the two of them singing karaoke, pictures of Ron, Maria, Stella and Jim playing pool with Bob at the Ring of Foreclosure, pictures of Zombie Howard Cosell mugging for the camera at VVVMC, and pictures of Ron Junior playing in his playpen.

Ron and Jim took their place near the stage of Carnaval Court while The Whipits broke into "Here Comes the Bride," 80s style. It sounded like Simon Le Bon of Duran Duran was getting married, Ron decided. He looked down at his white velour track suit; yep, Crockett and Tubbs would have been proud.

Maria and Stella started walking around the bar towards the stage; Stella was smoking a cigarette. Really? Ron thought. He glared at her.

"Oh, shit, dad, sorry," she said as the put the cigarette out on the stainless steel surface of the bar. As Stella and Maria entered his view, Ron realized that these two women, as opposite as they might be, were the two most important people in his life. He beamed as inside his body, his human heart swelled. His *human* heart. And this would be his *human* wife. Here he was, Ron Watson, piece of shit zombie, divorced and hit by a truck and left for dead on so many levels, getting a second chance in both life and in marriage. And he swore, right then, that he wouldn't fuck either life or marriage up. This was now his mission.

"Dearly beloved, we are gathered here today to get through this thing called marriage," Robyn said. She was dressed all in purple and had a unicorn horn on her head; she insisted that if the powers that be at the Church of the Purple Unicorn saw her perform a ceremony without those things she'd be excommunicated from the 'church.' And she had another wedding to perform for some friends in three weeks, so she needed to remain 'ordained.' For three more weeks, anyway.

"Mawwage," Stella said under her breath, quoting her favorite movie again, and Maria, Ron, and Jim all cracked up. Quietly, so they didn't disrupt Robyn, who was going through the vows she wrote. Ron didn't hear any of them because he spent the whole time staring into Maria's eyes, which were deep wells of blue understanding topped with a layer of passion and a dollop of wild and crazy, all things that Ron loved about her; her eyes sucked him in and he never wanted to leave…

"A TOAST!"

Ron looked around; who the fuck would want to toast before the vows were completed? What kind of a motherfucker would go that much out of order? Everybody knows that you toast AFTER the vows are completed, mostly because you were toasting the fact that the vows are completed. It's very helpful in long religious ceremonies where the priest/minister/rabbi/hired hand babbles on and on about Jesus and God and 'Love is patient, love is kind. It does not envy, it does not boast, blah blah blah.' Ron never understood why every wedding he ever went to had those same vows; didn't people get tired of hearing the same things over and over again? He always thought wedding vows should be more rock and roll. "Whole Lotta Love" by Led Zeppelin (by way of Willie Dixon) comes to mind: *You've been coolin', baby/I've been droolin'/all the good times I've been misusin'/way, way down inside/I'm gonna give you my love/I'm gonna give you every inch of my love/gonna give you my love.* Of course, when he suggested this idea to Maria, she said her song would be "Keep Your Hands To Yourself."

"Ron Watson." It sounded far away, so Ron looked over by the entrance to Harrah's. Nobody was over there except a fat dude… with a posse of zombies behind him. A zosse? Shit.

Ron looked closer; it was that motherfucker Portly Elvis. From the Bourbon Room Elvis Disaster. That was the night the Bourbon

Room was 'all shook up.' That was the night it became the 'Neck-break Hotel.' That was the night they all discovered that Portly Elvis was truly a 'Hound Dog.' Ron giggled at the Elvis jokes running through his head like fast Elvis cars on a clear Elvis highway.

"Ron Watson, we meet again." Portly Elvis was speaking through a megaphone; no wonder Ron could hear him but not see him. Hearing Portly Elvis before you saw Portly Elvis was unheard of without electronic assistance. Dude was huge.

"DAVID!" Sidney screamed and ran over and wrapped her arms around Portly Elvis. And then she backed away and threw up on the concrete apron surrounding Carnaval Court. "Holy shit, you stink!"

"Oh, hey, Portly Elvis, what's up?" Ron yelled. He was hoping that this fucktard and his zombie posse were just here to have some drinks or whatever; he surely wasn't invited to the wedding. They say 'keep your friends close and your enemies closer,' but inviting fucking Portly Elvis to his fucking wedding would be like keeping his fucking enemies in his fucking bed. And keeping a fucking toothbrush for his fucking enemies in his fucking bathroom medicine cabinet.

Ron also hoped Portly wasn't trying to cozy up to him for whatever reason; he really wasn't interested in having Portly Elvis apply to his zombie friend club. Dude had no fucking morals.

Portly Elvis approached Ron with his horde of zombies behind him. It was like there was an invisible fence keeping them behind PE. As they got closer, Ron realized they were the same zombies from the hospital and the same zombies from the car on the way to the hospital – one with the same 'Zombie Lounge' shirt on – and the same zombies who used to be KILLZ guys. Wait, what? He looked closer; yep, those were KILLZ zombies. Damn, two enemies in one. Shit.

And they were singing. Every last one of them. *When them zombies like to eat, you know they start on their feet, EVERYBODY*

GET YOUR GUNS AND LET'S MUNCH ON SOME HUMAN BUNS!

The gathered zombies swayed in unison as they sang. It was like watching the video for "We Are The World" except Lionel Richie, Cindy Lauper and Michael Jackson were zombie #1, zombie #2, and Michael Jackson. Ron did a double take; yep, that zombie standing right there, with his black fedora and his one glove and his red marching-band-like uniform was formerly a Michael Jackson impersonator. Either that or he ate a Michael Jackson impersonator and stole his clothes.

"I understand you're getting married today." Portly Elvis had ditched the megaphone, yet his booming voice filled the bar. Ron wondered why so many fat people had booming voices; perhaps their vocal cavities were as huge as their bellies? Perhaps they weren't actually fat, they were just cavernous? "I also understand I wasn't on the fucking guest list, asshole."

Behind Portly Elvis the KILLZ zombies made a sound. "Ooooooooooh," like the sound The Jerry Springer Show audience makes when the surprise cousin/lover/transvestite guest is brought out from behind the curtain to refute the charges that he/she/it cheated on whoever/whatever was already on stage.

"We threw it together kinda fast, and, uh…" Behind Ron, The Whipits and the Carnaval Court bartenders nonchalantly watched, like this was something that happened all the fucking time. Shootout at high noon, every fucking Tuesday at Carnaval Court.

"And you didn't have my e-mail, I'm sure, baby," Portly Elvis said with his best Elvis drawl.

"That's right, bitch, he didn't have your e-mail," Robyn said from the stage. "And he still doesn't have it. Now get lost so we can finish and these people can live happily ever after. Like they're supposed to."

"Not so fast, Missy," Portly Elvis said, as he drew a gun from inside his white polyester suit and pointed it at Robyn. "We're not here for your fucking wedding, or for your fucking purple unicorn bullshit – is that really a unicorn head on your human head?"

"Are you here for drinks?" Charlie asked, with a grin on his face. He always had a grin on his face, whether he was staring down a crazy zombie with a loaded weapon or holding hands with his girlfriend. Dude was happy.

"NO," Portly Elvis bellowed; his voice shook the roof. Dude could bellow.

Tony of The Whipits spoke into the stage microphone: "Are you here to dance? We can make you dance! A-one, a-two, a-three -"

Portly Elvis pointed his gun to the ceiling of Carnaval Court and shot one round, putting a hole above the second 'a' and making it look like 'Carnival Court,' which is how everybody spells it anyway. Americans aren't really known for knowing the proper names or pronunciations of foreign cities, countries or festivals.

"We're not here to fucking dance or sing or drink or fuck – We're here for the antidote," he bellowed again, like a manatee looking for a date across the Amazon.

"I wasn't offering to fuck you," Tony replied, nervously. From behind Portly Elvis a scream rose out of the crowd of zombies, which now appeared to be in the hundreds, according to Ron. They all screamed, in unison, in a high pitched voice that sounded like a witch being boiled alive, "ANNNNTTTTTTTTTIIIIIIIIDOOOOOOOTTTEEEE!"

"As you can tell, they're here for the same thing," Portly Elvis said, pointing behind him. "And we ain't leavin' until we get it." He waved the gun at Robyn, as if to remind her it was there. Pointed at her. Like it was about to kill a unicorn.

"Antidote? We don't have an antidote," Ron said, trying to delay the proceedings so he could figure out a way to end this and get back to his wedding, which, really, should have been the event of the day. Who the fuck tries to upstage a wedding? Portly Elvis fuck, that's who. Ron would have eaten him, but hey, wait a minute,

Ron was human now, and his conscience reminded him *You can't eat him, bitch, you're human.* He wasn't even hungry for the taste of human blood, anyway; no, he was hungry for a cheeseburger, and Maria had promised him that on their way to their honeymoon they could swing by In N Out over in the Linq to get a Double Double, Animal Style, with fries and a vanilla shake. And while you can upstage a wedding, Mister Portly Elvis Fuck, you can never upstage a human's desire for a Double Double, Animal Style.

Then it hit Ron: all he needed was a boombox and a copy of Michael Jackson's "Thriller." If he could get that going, the zombies would start dancing, right? And then he and his wedding party could run like hell, right?

"C'mere." The gun was now pointed at Ron's head, and, because he didn't quite yet have a viable plan – there were no boomboxes nearby – for getting rid of this douchecanoe and getting his Double Double, Animal Style, he did as he was told and moved closer to Portly Elvis. Shoot me, you fuck, he thought, and I'll fucking eat you. *But you're not a zombie anymore.* Shit. All of a sudden, Ron was a little worried, because humans don't take bullets to head very well. No, he thought, humans like bullets to the head about as well as Republicans like facts.

Portly Elvis grabbed Ron's right cheek with his thumb and forefinger, pinched, and pulled. "Owww! That fucking hurts, asshole," Ron said, as he twisted away and saw Maria in her sweet white wedding dress, standing next to Flippy, looking frightened. Fuck Portly Elvis; nobody makes my fiancee frightened. Ron realized he was going to have to think like a zombie to get out of this, not a human. First of all, if he was human, he'd have a gun, and he, Ron Watson, didn't have a gun. Yet. Tomorrow he was going to go fucking get one, he said to himself.

"See," Portly Elvis said, a sardonic grin crossing his face, like he had a secret that he was sleeping with Ron's mom or something. He pulled the zombie to his right close to him, grabbed his cheek, pinched and pulled, and the zombie didn't move. And Portly Elvis' hand was full of dead zombie skin. He pointed the gun at Ron's head. "You, sir, are a fucking human."

"Hey, wow, I guess I am," Ron said, still trying to figure out exactly how to get out of this dilemma. It was much easier to get out of dilemmas when you were a zombie; you just took a bite. When you were a human? *You should get a gun, bitch.* See? His conscience was right; that seemed to be the solution to most humanly dilemmas, but, being that he was a new human, he hadn't had time to procure a gun. Nor would he want one, really, on most days. On most days he was a pacifist, who believed that humans didn't have the capacity to regulate themselves with regard to guns, based on the number of shootings that happen all across the country every day, but when a man has his wedding day interrupted by a moron with a gun, his political views can change rather quickly. Tomorrow he was going to go fucking get a gun. Isn't that what every unarmed person said to themselves when they had a gun pointed at their head?

"And you became a human somehow. How, Ron?" Portly Elvis jiggled when he spoke. "How? Magic? Luck? Did you eat your Wheaties this morning?"

All the zombies behind Portly Elvis laughed. Really? A Wheaties joke is funny? Ron shook his head as the zombies high-fived each other. It was like watching a college fraternity of the damned. Instead of SAE or whatever, this fraternity might be called 666. Or SAD. Sigma Alpha Douchebag. Or WTF. Ron chuckled, as the barrel of Portly Elvis' gun pressed harder into his forehead.

"HOW, MOTHERFUCKER?" Portly Elvis was maybe getting a little frustrated with Ron's Sigma Alpha Douchebag flight of fancy. "I'LL TELL YOU HOW, MOTHERFUCKER. YOU HAVE THE ANTIDOTE. AND SHE MADE IT."

All of a sudden, the gun was pointed at Stella, who was standing next to her dad smoking a cigarette. Oh, no, Ron thought, you can point the gun at me all you want, but don't threaten my daughter. I'll eat you. *You can't eat him, bitch, you're human.* Ron pinched his left arm with his right hand; yep, his conscience was finally right. Is this what happened when you were human? Your conscience was always right? He remembered back to his days PZ – Pre-Zombie – when he was human, and nope, his conscience wasn't always right. If his conscience had been in charge of Ron not doing stupid shit, it wasn't very good at it. PZ. Back when he bailed on his ex-wife Erika and gave up on Stella and slutted up the entire western half of the USA on some pseudo-masculine attempt to prove his own virility to himself. His conscience sat that whole episode out.

But right now? Right now his conscience it was right on. He couldn't eat Portly Elvis because he was human. He looked Portly Elvis up and down; who the fuck would want to eat him anyway? Dude was huge. It would be like ordering a 16 ounce bone-in steak and having it show up as a 64 ounce steak which was actually 48 ounces of fat. Gross.

Portly Elvis cocked his gun. "I WILL KILL YOU RIGHT NOW, LITTLE LADY, IF YOU DON'T GIVE ME THE FUCK-ING ANTIDOTE."

For the first time that Ron could remember, Stella looked scared. She reached down her shirt and pulled out the vial on the necklace she was wearing and pulled it out and gave it to Portly Elvis.

"THIS IS IT?"

"It's very strong, sir. And that's," Stella started crying, "the last of it."

"Well, hello, beautiful," Portly Elvis said, as he and the other zombies around him eyed the vial. "Come to daddy."

Stella composed herself. "Why the fuck did you want the an-tidote," she asked, from beneath the barrel of the gun. "I mean, if you're going to turn all these guys," she waved her hand at the posse of zombies behind Portly Elvis, "back into humans, I would have given you the antidote. No need for a gun, although a 'please' might help. Bitch."

Portly Elvis pushed the barrel of his gun into Stella's forehead and Ron bared his teeth. *You can't eat him, bitch, yo –* SHUTUP, CONSCIENCE. I'LL BE A CANNIBAL TO SAVE MY DAUGHTER.

"Well, honey," Portly Elvis said, looking at Stella like she was his next meal, "if you must know, we're going to destroy it." He threw the vial onto the ground and stepped on it; liquid and smoke wafted out from underneath his size 13 blue suede shoes.

"Interrrrresting," Stella said, as she slowly moved the barrel of the gun to the side and put her hand on Portly Elvis' belly. It wasn't hard to do; the thing was right in front of her. Hell, his belly was so big it was right in front of everybody in Las Vegas. Ron gagged as Stella continued. "Why, big boy, would you destroy it? Don't all these guys," she said, pointing at the zombies behind Portly Elvis, "want to be human?"

"Well, darlin'..." Portly Elvis put his hand over Stella's hand as as she smiled sweetly at him and bile rose in Ron's throat. "If you must know, and since I'm gonna kill you anyway, I'll tell you why." Stella and Ron, his lips holding back vomit, glanced at each other furtively, as Ron thought, kill us anyway? What the fuck? "Me and my associates here are the owners of Zombie Bay," Portly Elvis continued, his chest puffed out like a peacock, "which has made us extremely wealthy – *extremely* wealthy – have you noticed the rhinestones on my jumpsuit? – and if this antidote gets out, all of our volunteer zombie workers will want it and all of the zombies all over the world will want it and poof! Business plan up in smoke. And Zombie Bay has made us *extremely* wealthy and makes us more *extremely* wealthy every day."

"Isn't Zombie Bay the one where the zombies ate everybody?" Jim had sidled up to the conversation.

"No, dumbass," Portly Elvis replied, his gun now pointing at Jim, "That was Zombie Island Resort. That place was so mismanaged."

"All those zombies work for us now," a zombie to Portly Elvis' right said. He was wearing a blue pinstripe suit and tie; juxtaposed with his rotting face and skin dangling from his ear, it was as surreal a sight as Ron could remember seeing.

Portly Elvis turned his gun back to Stella now. "They *do* work for us. And they don't eat tourists anymore; it attracts too much attention."

"That's right," his nattily dressed zombie associate said. "Ever since we started Human Farms, we've had plenty to feed these guys without attracting attention."

"Human farms?" Stella asked.

"Have you noticed how you never hear from politicians who lose elections?"

Ron thought for a second; he was right. "Yeah."

"Human farms," Portly Elvis' associate said, as a piece of his skin fell off and he adjusted his tie. "They are fucking delicious. You should try a failed Green Party Presidential candidate sometime."

"They're organic," Portly Elvis said.

"Wow," Stella said, her face a pastiche of shock and awe.

"We're doing so well we're going to open Zombie Bays in Atlantic City," Portly Elvis said.

"Take over the Mohegan Sun in Connecticut," his zombie associate said.

"And Foxwoods."

"Chumash."

"Pechanga. The Native Americans love us!"

"We're going to open one in Paris, call it Euro Zombie Bay!"

"Do you really think that's a good idea," Ron asked. "Isn't Euro Disney a disaster, financially?"

"FUCK YOU," Portly Elvis said, his gun now pointing at Ron. "ZOMBIES WILL RULE THE WORLD!"

All the zombies behind Portly Elvis laughed and screeched and Ron recognized the sound. It was the same sound he heard on his way to the hospital, coming from that Firebird that pulled up next to Stella's El Camino.

"Are you the only one who knows how to make the antidote?" Portly Elvis asked Stella, standing there in her Debbie Harry t-shirt and her black jeans.

"Duh," Stella said, with a smirk. "Who the fuck else would be able to come up with such a thing? Surely not you." It was the wrong time to be sassy, Ron thought. It was like telling your future boss at your job interview that his wife is a hag; a bangable hag, but still a hag. It was like telling your future wife on your first date that she has cankles. It was like telling your archenemy that he was a moron.

Which is exactly what Stella did.

Portly Elvis pointed his gun at her. "Then I'm going to have to kill you."

"Whoa, whoa, wait a minute," Ron said, frantically searching for an escape route in his head. His human brain sure wasn't as devious or as clever as his zombie brain was; if he was still a zombie he would have put football field chalk on his face and snuck everybody out or something.

"I can't have her making any more antidote and ruining my empire, bitch," Portly Elvis said, sounding a lot like Ron's own conscience. "So she must die." He pulled the trigger of his gun and Ron did the only thing he could think of with his human brain; he pushed Stella out of the way and, in the process, took the bullet right in his chest. It hurt as much as a Republican accepting facts…and much, much worse. Ron could feel his heart explode and, as he lost consciousness and fell to the concrete floor of Carnaval Court, he saw his life flash before his eyes…his life that was only three days old.

CHAPTER
21

Ron – Human?
Maria – Human.
Stella – Young Adult.
Jim – Human.
Ron Junior – Toddler.

Ron awoke in a pool of sweat. On an airplane. What the fuck? An airplane? He was in a window seat and looked out; the sun sat low on the horizon like a whole egg yolk in a pan. He swiveled and realized he was sitting next to Maria, who was holding Ron Junior. Next to her was Stella, and in the seat across the aisle sat Jim. A bored voice came on the airplane cabin's speakers.

"Annnnnnnd this is yourrrrrrrrrr captain, we've reached cruising altitude so sit back, relax, and thank you for flying Zombie Airliiiiiiiiiiines. Where flying doesn't cost you an arm and a leg."

WHAT.

THE.

FUCK.

"Hi beautiful," Maria said as she stroked Ron's cheek and pulled a piece of skin off of it.

A piece of skin.

Fuck, he was a zombie again. Motherfuckers. After all that he had been through, with the Nutella and the pink penis and the best seven seconds of his life and his brilliant daughter creating the antidote, he was a zombie again? MOTHERFUCKERS. Somebody was going to pay.

"I'm a zombie again, right?"

"You were a few minutes ago but Flippy gave you some antidote."

Ron lifted his right arm; yep, it worked. He was human. Oh, wow! He was human again! Okay, so maybe the motherfuckers weren't so bad after all, right? The skin off of his face must have been left over from a few minutes ago, right?

Then he remembered what happened at his wedding. "Antidote? I thought we gave that to Portly Elvis?"

Stella popped up in her chair to look at Ron around Maria. "We did, dad, but we sure as fuck didn't give him ALL of it. That would have been stupid. The rest of it is in our luggage." Her black makeup had run down her face like she had been crying. "Good to see you back, dad. We were worried for a minute."

"Dad daa. DADDAAAA," Ron Junior said with conviction, his bright blue eyes looking deep into Ron's soul. Then he farted and giggled and squirmed in Maria's arms like a handful of wet farting squirming spaghetti noodles.

"His first word, honey!" Maria looked at Ron Junior. "Your first word is DADDDAA!"

"DADAAA!" Ron said, smiling.

"DADAAAA!" Maria repeated.

"DADAAAA" Ron Junior said and kicked the seat in front of him. A head lifted up from the seat, turned around, and it was Portly Elvis.

"Oh, fuck, you again?" Ron asked.

"I heard what you said, little lady. I figured that wasn't all of the antidote, so after that little dust-up at Carnaval Court I followed you. And here we are. Oh, and I might have accidentally turned your friends into zombies. Sorry about that." Portly Elvis shrugged. "Collateral damage and all that."

"You fucker," Stella said.

"FUCKK-KKKER," Ron Junior said, with spit running down the side of his chin. His second word!

"You turned my friends into zombies?" Ron was having trouble remembering anything from the time he got shot until the time he woke up on this fucking airplane, so his questions were going to be rudimentary compared to everybody else's.

"Yeah, accidentally." Portly Elvis made air quotes with his fingers as he said 'accidentally' and Ron wished he had a gun. Again.

"Sorry about that. They were in my way." Portly Elvis laughed and it was the laugh of an evil fat zombie who knew he was an evil fat zombie. "Now, about the antidote."

"Can I get you anything to drink?" A flight attendant, 'Lynda' by her name tag, was standing at the end of their aisle. A piece of skin was dangling from her face, so she was obviously a zombie flight attendant, but Ron noticed that she was gorgeous. Tall and graceful, with long brown hair, a smile loaded with sunshine, and flawless what-remained-of-her-zombie-skin. As she turned to get out of the way of a passenger heading to the forward restroom, Ron also noticed that her ass was resplendent in her tight black Zombie Airlines flight attendant dress. He realized this was the first time he ever found himself, as a human, attracted to a zombie, and wondered what this said about his mental state. And about the state of the universe. Clearly, it was fucked up.

"I'd like a coke, please," Maria said from the middle seat, where she was holding Ron Junior, who was now fast asleep. And that's when the whole world went to shit. Again.

"ALRIGHT, LISTEN UP, THIS IS YOURRRRRRRRRRRRR CAPTAIN, AND DUE TO SOME LITTLE FUCKING JOAN JETT SHIT GIRL BRINGING ILLEGAL SUBSTANCES ON THIS

PLANE WE'RE GOING TO CRASH IT. SO SIT BACK, RELAX, AND PREPARE TO DIE, COURTESY OF ZOMBIE AIRLINES. THAAAAAAAT'S, RIGHT, DIE. IF YOU LOOK OUT THE RIGHT SIDE OF THE PLANE, YOU'LL SEE UTAH, WHERE WE'RE GOING TO CRASH AND YOU'RE GOING TO DIE. UNLESS, OF COURSE, YOU'RE ALREADY A ZOMBIE, THEN LET'S PARTAAAAAAAY!"

Portly Elvis looked at Stella as the plane lurched downward. "He's talking about you." That same fucking bro-country zombie song that Ron heard on the way to the hospital started playing over the airplane speakers and the plane dove like it was a roller coaster going over the first huge hill of its tracks. And Portly Elvis sang along….

"…When them zombies like to eat you know they start on the feet EVERYBODY GET YOUR GUNS AND LET'S MUNCH ON SOME HUMAN BUNS…."

Fuck me, Ron thought, the guy singing on the radio WAS Portly Elvis. He KNEW IT!

This couldn't end well.

"Surprised?" Portly Elvis asked in his distinctive Elvis-like drawl. Ron thought that if this Elvis had an Elvistory, it would end with Ron killing him. Somehow, someway.

Ron Junior sighed; at least he was asleep despite the horrible country zombie song blaring over the descending airplane's speakers. Maria and Stella lurched forward in their seats, their seat belts holding them in. Good thing they watched the fucking safety demonstration before the plane took off so they knew how to buckle those complicated buckles, Ron thought. He never understood why they always showed that particular part of the safety demonstration, because didn't everybody know how to buckle a buckle? But now, finally, he got it. As his own seat belt strained against his abdomen but kept him from crashing into the seat in front of him, he got it.

"Shit," Maria said, as Ron Junior sighed again. She looked at Ron with a look that said she was tired of this roller coaster ride.

"Dad, we gotta do something," Stella said, her eyes wide. "All these people are going to die!" Ron looked around; every other passenger on the plane was up out of their seats, dancing to the song. They were all motherfucking zombies, and none of them were going to die, because they were already dead.

"Um, I think they're already dead, honey," Ron said, a smirk on his face that said, 'Hey, sometimes the dad *is* smarter than the teenaged daughter!'

"Fuck, I thought they were humans when they got on," Stella said, anger on her face that said, 'Dad, you're never smarter than your teenaged daughter. In fact, you're never smarter than your newborn son. Asshole.' Ron wondered how he could see the word 'asshole' so clearly on her face without it being spelled out…then he remembered she was his daughter, which means she was a product of his ex-wife Erika…and he could always see the word 'asshole' clearly on Erika's face.

Ron looked closely at a dancing zombie near him and recognized football field chalk on his face and a piece of "Ron Zombie" duct tape on his face. Yep, these were zombies and yep, they were on this plane with his family.

ZOMBIES WERE ON THIS MOTHERFUCKING PLANE WITH HIS FAMILY.

This plane, which was going to crash.

GOING TO MOTHERFUCKING CRASH, RON!

Ron quickly stood up to go to the front of the plane, where he was going to pull some heroic shit and be a motherfucking hero by grabbing the controls of the plane and flying it until it safely landed in Denver, because he had seen all kinds of action movies and this was how it always turned out, right? Yippy kie yay motherfuckers? And whatnot?

Except, he realized, he didn't know how to fly a plane. Still, no matter, it was time to be an American Badass and save his family and all these zombies from certain death by plane crash...except the zombies were already dead, so fuck them, but he was definitely going to save his fucking family! He was Ron Zombie, bitches, and he was an American Badass and it was time to GET IT ON! MOTHERFUCKERS!

Except, he realized, he had run right into the chest of Portly Elvis, which, being that he was portly, was more like running into a fucking tank, except it was a jiggly tank full of fat from many years of overeating and zero years of exercising. And he was an entire aisle wide. He also realized Portly Elvis' chest wasn't moving, which unfortunately impeded his ability to get his family to safety. Fucking impediments.

"I HAVE HAD IT WITH THESE MOTHERFUCKING HIN-DRANCES ON THIS MOTHERFUCKING PLANE," Ron said, way too loud, as the plane continued its nose-dive towards certain death. The zombies thought that was the funniest fucking thing anybody had ever said and laughed....all at the same time. It was the same laugh Ron heard from the Firebird on the way to the hospital. More like a screech, like the sound of 8,473 nails on 2,899 chalkboards. More like torture, like the sound of somebody shoving the actual Eiffel Tower up a man's ass. More like the sound of duct tape being ripped from somebody's testicles without regard for human capacity for pain. Again.

It was the sound of the humans on the plane dying. Again.

And not because they were being eaten by the zombies. No. Portly Elvis said as much. "The song makes them un-hungry, if that's a word," he said, as he noticed Ron's face wondering about such an event. "I control them." A pause the size of the San An-dreas fault opened up in the plane and Portly Elvis lifted his hands up to the sky as if to summon his own unholy apparition from on high. "Surprised, bitches?"

As the 757 bound for Denver made its damned way towards the Utah desert, literally, Ron balled up his right fist, which he was only able to do because he was human again, hurtled it towards Portly Elvis' massive and ugly face, and OW! FUCK! THAT FUCKING HURTS!

"You stupid human bitch," Portly Elvis said, in his nasally Southern accent, as Ron grabbed his fist and winced. "That shit hurts when you're a human, doesn't it?" Portly Elvis reached up and touched his face; a crater lived where Ron's fist had landed. "Even when you put a hole in my fucking face. Bitch." He reared back and hit Ron square in the face. DOWN GOES WATSON! DOWN GOES WATSON!

Ron awoke, on the ground, face up, sand on his cheek, to the smell of burning flesh, burning electronics, and burning cactus. Shit. He was getting tired of waking up in strange places; sure, when he was in his 20s he might get drunk and wake up in strange beds from time to time, but at least he knew he was in a bed. It was much weirder to wake up on an airplane or to the smell of things burning or the sound of a crying baby. A crying baby? Fuck. He opened his eyes to see Ron Junior staring him in the face, crying, Ron's arms grasping him as tight as a rusted lug nut on a 1974 Plymouth Roadrunner. "Dada," Ron Junior said through his tears, and Ron felt his heart well up, because while he smelled burning flesh and electronics, he knew his son was safe, which was a moment that would make most human beings cry profusely...but for Ron, no tears came.

"You're a zombie now," a voice said, over his left shoulder. Ron tilted his head back to see Lynda, the flight attendant, with blood dripping down her chin. She smiled. Ron frowned.

"I'm..........so...............confused," Ron said, forcing the words out as quickly as his brain could process them. Fuck, maybe he *was* a zombie again. Could this be true? What happened to the antidote? The Nutella? STELLA?

Lynda wiped her chin with her bare left arm. Wait, wasn't that supposed to be covered with her flight attendant uniform? "The plane crashed and you and your friends died, but I bit you all and turned you into zombies."

"Thank........you." Ron was having all kinds of trouble getting his words out, but he sure remembered his manners. His momma would be so proud.

"Dad." Ron turned his head to his right as Ron Junior giggled atop him. He saw Stella laying on the ground amidst smoking plan parts and bodies. She turned her head to him; "DAD."

"You're.....okay?"

"Okay," she replied. "Junior?"

Ron looked at Ron Junior, he looked like he was still human, somehow, and didn't have a scratch on him. "Okay. Maria?"

Maria was still strapped to her seat, and her seat was on the ground so she was okay. She looked like she was riding the entire earth, a direct flight to hell. "I'm fine, you guys. Barely a scratch. I'm not a zombie either, but Lynda saved the rest of you."

"Good," Ron said. That was everybody...hey, wait a minute! "Jim?"

"JIM?" Stella slowly moved her head around. "JIM?"

"He didn't make it," Lynda said, pointing towards where the fuselage of the plane was stuck into the ground nose first, like a giant was playing in a sandbox and left his shovel behind. The fuselage was smoking and half of it had disintegrated, as if into thin air. Stella began to cry, but no tears came because she was a zombie. It was a dry cry, and it was the first time Stella had ever been a zombie, so Ron could see that she was confused.

"So.....confused.....brains." Stella heard what she herself just said and screamed long and hard like she was falling down a well to China.

Ron stood up slowly, keeping Ron Junior in his arms, and shuffled over to Stella. "Brai....honey."

"Brains," Stella repeated. "Fuck!" She stared up into her father's eyes, her face a coagulation of fear, sadness, and apoplectic rage. Ron was familiar with the rage part, but he wasn't sure he had ever seen fear or sadness on his daughter's face before. Sure, it didn't help that he wasn't around for all those awkward pre-teen years, but still. Stella as a human was much tougher than Stella as a zombie. Ironically.

Ron knelt down next to her and brushed her bloody zombie hair from her bloody zombie face. He looked into her deep, black, confused zombie eyes.

"Love," he said, pointing to himself and then to her. Maria had gotten herself out of her seat (thanks to the pre-flight safety demonstration showing her how to undo the belt buckle!) and was standing behind Ron.

"Love," she said, pointing to herself and then to Stella.

"Lub," Ron Junior said, from Ron's arms, as his arms flailed about and he pointed at everything. His lub, as was everybody's, was for everything.

"LUB," they all said, together, as the plane smoldered around them and Lynda the flight attendant offered them all airplane blankets. This was going to be a long night and airplane blankets were the last vestige of a formerly normal world. Despite the blood and the carnage and the fact that Jim was gone and that everybody else except Maria and Ron Jr. were zombies, they spread the airplane blankets out and slept on the desert floor...in the shape of a pentagram.

CHAPTER
22

Ron – Zombie or human? Who knows?
Maria – Human.
Stella – Zombie and Not Lovin' It.
Jim – Dead.
Ron Junior – Toddler.

Ron awoke, on the ground, face up, to the sun in his face, to the sand in his pants, and to the sounds of a sleeping child. Which is to say, silence. What the fuck? Waking up in a strange place AGAIN? This was getting old. Ron couldn't wait until the day he woke up in the apartment he shared with Maria.

Maria!

He tilted his head to the right and got a faceful of sand. Dammit, this meant he was either in the desert…or back in 3rd grade, where Erin Irwin would push his face down in the sandbox at lunch, no matter if the fucking lunch lady was watching or not. Fucking lunch lady was in Erin Irwin's back pocket. She had to be. Why else would the fucking lunch lady not stop Erin Irwin from kicking Ron Watson's ass every day at lunch? Erin Irwin was a fucking asshole and everybody at Silver Wing Elementary knew it, everybody except the fucking lunch lady.

He opened his eyes; no Erin Irwin anywhere. Fuck, he was in the desert. And even though it was morning, he could feel the rhythm of the heat. Heat....hot...enough to knock a zombie out. Again.

He awoke again, sitting up in the passenger seat of a pink 1972 Monte Carlo with rusty chrome rims, one leg out the window, his arms tightly around Ron Junior. Fuck this falling asleep shit, he thought. All of a sudden, he longed for the days when he was a zombie and never slept. He looked at his the index finger and noticed there was no skin on it, just exposed, bloody bone.

Fuck.

He *was* a zombie.

All this falling asleep/taking antidote/passing out/crashing airplanes was getting confusing; was he zombie or human? Who knew?

"Dad....BRAINS."

He turned his head to see Stella's head, bloody and ripped apart like a package delivered to your front door by a carrier who didn't give a shit, right in front of his own face, as if though she were playing defensive tackle and the football was about to be snapped. A hand reached over from the driver's seat and pushed Stella's head back into the rear of the Monte Carlo, and Ron could see that Maria was driving the car. And that Stella was in the back seat of the car. And that there was a window between the front and back seats...so Ron reached over and closed it.

And locked it.

And from behind the window, Ron could hear Stella's muffled cries.

"BRRRRRNNNNNS."

"She's having a little trouble adapting," Maria said, and took a hit off of a cigarette.

Maria didn't smoke.

What the fuck?

"You're brains?" Ron asked.

Fuck. Was he missing words again?

"Smoking? Shit, Ronnie baby, wouldn't you? I'm in a fucking rustbucket and I've gotta get my human son and my zombie husband and step-daughter back to Vegas as fast as possible. Of course I'm smoking."

Ron looked out the window to see cactus rushing past him like they were trying to escape Nevada. Stupid cactus. Who would want to escape Nevada?

As the pink Monte Carlo gobbled up miles of pavement like Miss Pac-Man gobbling up those little yellow dots she liked to eat – were they nutritious? Were they delicious? As a 16-year-old boy, these were the kinds of questions Ron Watson asked at the arcade. And yes, it did get his ass kicked, thanks for asking – it all came back to him slowly; the plane flight, the crash, the sleeping in the desert, the racing back to Las Vegas.

Wait, why the fuck were they going *back* to Las Vegas?

"BRRNNNNNNNNNNNNS" from the back of the Monte Carlo.

"Why back?" he asked, but it really came out more like "Wh-hhhh bllllllh."

"What, honey?" Maria asked, and took another hit off of her cigarette.

The cadence of the highway calmed Ron for a second as he considered where he was. He looked to his right and saw nothing, just vast expanses of sand and sky. If there were an ocean nearby this would be an upper class vacation destination.

And if Ron were human he could talk.

And if Portly Elvis were nice he wouldn't be trying to run their Monte Carlo off the road right now with his Mustang II, his distorted orange face leering out the window at Ron like Donald Trump about to grab a hot 24-year-old blonde woman by her pussy.

The Mustang II – one of the worst attempts to update a muscle car, in Ron's opinion, because it didn't look like a Mustang at all, it looked like the unwanted baby that resulted when a 1968 Mustang GT fucked a 1974 AMC Pacer – scraped against the Monte Carlo on the right side, Ron's side, and the Monte Carlo swerved to its left.

What the actual fuck?

Maria tossed her cigarette out her open window and corrected the Monte Carlo so it was going forward again. "You again?" She then did something that endeared her to Ron even more, if that was possible: She proudly flew her middle finger at full staff, so Portly Elvis could see it. "Fuck you, you fucking fuck!"

Ron had not really heard Maria use such brilliant language and, frankly, it made his eyes go wide and gave him a bit of an erection. The next words she said didn't, though.

"Hold on."

Ron looked over at her; yep, she was serious. The short time that they had been together had taught him that face. He tightened his grip on Ron Junior. She turned the steering wheel sharply to the right and crashed the Monte Carlo into the Mustang II, sending it veering off the road, right into the desert. She gunned the Monte Carlo…and it ran out of gas.

As the Monte Carlo lurched and stumbled to a slow death, the Mustang II – which, Ron revised, looked like a car centipede with a 1968 Mustang GT and a 1974 AMC Pacer and the devil himself, all locked together in ass-to-mouth hell – came up to the right of them and slowed. Portly Elvis turned to Ron and flew his own middle finger at the Monte Carlo.

"Fuck you, you fucking fucks!"

"Wow," Ron said to Maria, who was flying her own middle finger back at Portly Elvis. "The two of you speak the brains language."

"You fuckface," Maria yelled to Portly Elvis as the Monte Carlo sighed, a car on its last fumes. "You better not hurt them."

Hurt who, Ron thought. He looked around; Ron Junior, Stella, and Maria were with him, and Jim was dead, so hurt who?

"Ha, little lady," Portly Elvis said with a ghastly smile that suggested a macabre carnival clown. "We aren't going to hurt them. We're going to kill them. The Portly Elvistory doesn't include them! HAHAHAHA!" The Mustang II gunned its engines and Ron heard that sound again; the sound of the end of the world. He looked over and saw that a back window in the Mustang II was rolled down and that the Mustang II was full of zombies. Laughing zombies. Zombies from the Zombie Lounge. He shuddered; even though a zombie shouldn't be wary of other zombies, this was not your ordinary every day zombie encounter. If zombies were with Portly Elvis, they were definitely bad zombies. And they were definitely bad news. So bad that one of them had a gun, pointed right at Ron.

Ron and Maria both ducked and avoided the shot from the gun, which passed through the Monte Carlo harmlessly. The Mustang II took off, its wheels squealing along the pavement, its engine backfiring, leaving a mark that looked like Ron Junior had taken a big long shit in his underwear. Sure, he wasn't old enough to wear underwear yet, but Ron surmised that one day he'd appreciate that joke.

"Kill who brains?" Ron still wasn't sure what the hell was going on. But his language abilities were quickly improving.

"SHIT FUCK ASS MOTHERFUCK COCKSUCKER SON OF A MOTHERLESS GOAT."

"BRAINS," Stella said. Between his wife and his daughter, Ron was sure his own vocabulary seemed normal.

"JUDAS PRIEST. MOTORHEAD. THE SCORPIONS. VAN HALEN BEFORE SAMMY FUCKING HAGAR." Maria was pounding the steering wheel of the pink Monte Carlo, screaming what sounded like names of heavy metal bands. Ron was so proud. Or something.

"BRAINS!" Stella said, muffled behind the glass behind Ron.

"Kill who?" Ron asked to the air. He wasn't sure either of his companions had their shit together enough to answer his question, but he thought it still should be out there.

Maria lifted her head up, grabbed a cigarette from the driver side door, lit it with a lighter, and took a drag. Then she turned to Ron and uttered the seven words Ron never wanted to hear, either in his life or in his death. The seven words that, for Ron, in any state, meant one thing: WAR.

"He's going to blow up Carnaval Court."

Ron's brain went cold, like it was trapped under three feet of ice. The chill enveloped him, engulfed him...enraged him. He felt a sharp pain in his right temple.

"And kill all of your friends."

"He already did." His temple throbbed.

"He turned them into zombies. But if he blows up Carnaval Court..."

"Why...he want to do that?" He reached up to his temple to massage it 'cuz it fucking hurt.

"The antidote."

"Antidote?" His finger on his temple felt something wet.

"They make the antidote in a lab underneath Carnaval Court. If we can get there in time, we can use it. And save everybody."

Ron felt dizzy, like he was about to pass out. His head fell to the side...and he felt something hot on his hand. He brought his hand down. Blood. Wait a minute, Ron thought, I'm a zombie I don't blee –

And with that, Ron Watson died again, for the last time, in a pink 1973 Monte Carlo going zero miles per hour through the Utah desert.

CHAPTER
23

Ron – Dead.
Maria – Human.
Stella – Zombie and Still Not Lovin' It.
Jim – Dead.
Ron Junior – Toddler.

Maria was not typically an overly emotional woman. She grew up the daughter of two math teachers, and the only emotion she saw in her childhood environment was mild elation when somebody was able to solve an algebra equation…and show their work. Other than that her childhood was logical, lucid, and coherent. And when she was a young adult she rebelled against that, which explained how she ended up hooking in Las Vegas. But still, even when she was making bad decisions, she was able to keep her emotions under control and lucid. It was ingrained in her, like her love of muscle cars and karaoke.

But when she got to Carnaval Court and it was gone, she sobbed. Uncontrollably. It was a reaction she was wholly unprepared for, because it was not lucid. In fact, it was as far away from lucid as you could get. It was anti-lucid. It was incoherent and illogical.

"WAAAAAAAAAAAAAAAAAH" she cried.

"WAAAAAAAAAAAAAAAH" Ron Junior cried. Ron's second home, Carnaval Court, the bar where Rob, Flippy, Charlie, Vache, Robyn and The Whipits were a family to Ron, Jim and Maria, lay in smoldering ruins around them, and Maria and Ron Junior had the exact same anti-lucid reaction. Or maybe Ron Junior was just hungry. She pulled the bottle of formula out of her Exene Cervenka t-shirt sleeve – she kept it rolled up in there, like a greaser or like Stella with her cigarettes – and fed Ron Junior.

And considered her options.

Ron was dead.

Jim was dead.

Stella was a zombie, wandering around Las Vegas after Maria let her out of the car and Stella tried to bite her.

Carnaval Court lay in ruins, its stainless steel bar top glistening in the Las Vegas late-day sun, its stage on fire. Maria could see body parts in the rubble; a hand here, a name tag there. She wondered how many of the bartenders and Whipits were there when the whole thing came down…and how many of them were already zombies…and what would become of them. She imagined they were all there, given that it was a Friday afternoon and Friday afternoons were usually pretty busy at the Court. That's what you called it when you were a regular there, The Court.

Were a regular.

There would be no regulars any more.

And how many tourists were in that rubble? She saw Hawaiian shirts, bachelorette party tank tops, and bartender uniforms.

Bartender uniforms. Covered in blood and tendons and entrails.

They were probably all dead. Really dead.

All dead.

Really dead.

Ron.

Jim.

Rob.

Charlie.

Robyn.

Flippy.

Vache.

The Whipits.

Sid.

Athena.

Crystal.

This world.

Through the bleakness of it all, through the haze of darkness that engulfed her soul, there was a light and Maria had a moment of clarity. She knew what she was going to do.

She was going to kill herself.

First she was going to leave Ron Junior with somebody who could take care of him. Then she was gonna kill herself.

No, first she was going to make sure he didn't have a poopy diaper. Then she was going to feed him a bottle of formula, so he wasn't hungry. Then she was going to kill herself.

No, then she was going to make sure he had his Ron Zombie blankie and his rattle. Then she was going to make cute little faces at him, like parents do, and get him to smile and coo and maybe spit up some of his formula onto himself. The she was going to laugh and make him giggle and then she was going to clean the formula off of his cute little Ron Zombie onesie, the one with the his father's bloody visage on the front, and then she was going to kiss him one time. And then she was going to get carried away and she was going to smack her lips and pretend to sneeze and tickle his rotund little belly until his belly shook like a bowlful of jelly and his mouth shrieked like a wolf.

And then she was going to kill herself.

CHAPTER
24

Ron – Dead?
Maria – Human.
Stella – Zombie.
Jim – Dead.
Ron Junior – Toddler.

Ron awoke in a hotel room, lying on a bed. He couldn't move his body, but his brain was awake. Small victories, right?

He looked around; it looked like every other hotel room in Las Vegas. He saw smoke outside the window and through the smoke he saw the giant behemoth of a Ferris wheel outside of Linq…so he knew he was at Harrah's.

At least he wasn't dead, right? At least not all the way. Maybe he was mostly dead, but mostly dead isn't all dead. Right?

He looked down at his arm; yep, the skin was gone, so he was a zombie.

Still.

He reached up to his head; yep, there was blood, so he was definitely shot.

In the head.

But he was not dead.

Whaddya say, Fred? Yeah, sometimes Ron's head liked to rhyme, even in the darkest hours. He didn't try to stop it because it made him laugh, bringing light to the darkness that seemed to engulf his life – or death – from time to time. He was a big believer in the light of comic relief, as if that wasn't obvious up to this point.

He was shot in the head, yet he was still a zombie, yet he could not move. This might have been the weirdest situation Ron had ever found himself in. And that was saying a hell of a lot, considering what Ron had been through recently.

On the bed next to him Ron found a note. "Good luck finding your friends in the rubble, fuckface," it said. "The Portly Elvistory doesn't include you or your fucking friends." Signed by Portly Elvis. Great.

The door to the hotel room opened and Maria ran in, furiously. Before she could see Ron she turned and sat down at the meager desk by the front door.

And pulled out a pistol.

Ron watched as she held the gun in her hands tentatively, as if though it were a new lover.

He tried to call out but could only grunt. Shit, he was a new zombie.

Again.

She rolled the pistol over in her hands, as if though she were considering its heft.

Smoke continued to arise outside the window.

Ron grunted.

Maria bit her lower lip and looked out the window.

Sentences began to form in Ron's mind.

She took the pistol and lifted it slowly towards her face.

Ron's synapses connected and fired like a domino run.

She stuck the barrel of the gun in her mouth and then pulled it out again.

Neuron junctions formed in Ron's brain.

She stuck the barrel of the gun back into her mouth.

Ron watched her, the love of his life, the mother of his child – where was Ron Junior? Didn't matter right now, Ron knew that she would have left him somewhere safe – the most beautiful creature, inside and out, he had ever been with, and he knew he couldn't let this happen. He couldn't live without her, no matter what state of "living" he would be in.

So he said the only thing he could think of.

"There's a shortage of perfect breasts in this world, t'would be a pity to ruin yours," he said, from his hotel room bed.

Maria turned, the pistol still in her mouth, and shrieked. She put the gun down and came over to Ron and started kissing his face, over and over and over again.

"Oh, Ron, will you ever forgive me?" she asked.

"What hideous sin have you committed lately?" Ron replied. His words and memory were coming quickly to him now.

"I got you killed. By a bullet from Portly Elvis' gun while we were stranded. Remember?"

"Never happened."

"What?"

"Never happened."

"But it did. I was there. Portly Elvis shot you and you died and I brought you to this hotel room."

"But I'm not dead. Wouldn't you agree, Your Portliness?" Portly Elvis appeared in the door of the hotel room.

"A technicality that will shortly be remedied," Portly Elvis said, with a sneer. "Why are we fucking quoting the Princess Bride?"

"I'll explain," Ron said, "and I'll use small words so that you'll be sure to understand, you warthog-faced buffoon."

"That literally may be the first time in my undead life a man has dared insult me," Portly Elvis said, and drew his own pistol, pointing it at Ron. "Get out of that bed so I can kill you properly, mano y mano. I would never shoot a man in bed."

"He can't get out of bed," Maria said.

"She's right," Ron said.

"Then we are at an impasse," Portly Elvis said, with a sigh. "However, I think you're bluffing," he continued, a smirk on his face the size of the Grand Canyon.

Ron's synapses had connected, his neurons had gathered into little neuronic communities, and his body? It was strong. Like ox.

"Or am I?" He slowly stood, to his feet, and brought the 'Ron Zombie' model AK-47 he found in his hotel room up, aiming it at Portly Elvis. He was all of a sudden ecstatic that Americans were gun happy, because whoever was in this hotel room last had left his souvenir AK-47, adorned with Ron's face on its stock. The occupant probably had a whole arsenal, since it was legal to do so, and didn't realize he had left one behind when he checked out. Ron realized he wouldn't be surprised if the Harrah's Lost and Found Room looked like an armory. He also realized he wouldn't be surprised if every gun in that armory had his face on it. Souvenir guns had become a big part of his merchandising empire, despite the fact that he was opposed to them and had not explicitly agreed to lend his likeness to weapons. Something about contract loopholes, his agent Dave had said. Despite Ron's opposition, however, the money from the sales was going to pay for Stella to go to a university, for Ron and Maria to buy a sweet house out in the Ring of Foreclosure, and much of it would be donated to firearm education organizations in Las Vegas, so Ron's conscience, as much as it could be, was mostly okay with it. Especially right now.

Aiming his AK-47 at Portly Elvis, right between the eyes, Ron said, slowly and deliberately, so as to show as much faux fierceness as possible, "DROP. YOUR. GUN."

Portly Elvis dropped his pistol.

"Have a seat."

Portly Elvis sat in the rickety wooden chair by the window of the hotel room. It collapsed and he crumpled to the floor like an unwanted towel after a shower.

"Have the next seat, you dumb fuck," Ron said, and pointed to the less-rickety chair right next to the broken rickety chair. Portly Elvis wobbled himself up, like a toddler sorta-succesfully learning to walk, and collapsed into the less-rickety chair.

"Tie him up," Ron said to Maria. "Make it as tight as you like. Remember, he did kill me. A couple of times."

Maria started tying Portly Elvis to the chair, as Ron sat back down on the bed. He had showed fierceness to get the job done, but now he needed to rest. Since he was shot and all.

Stella entered the room, holding Ron Junior, looking for all the world like a human girl. It was the gait; Ron had become quite adept at telling the difference between a zombie gait – slow, shuffling, plodding – and a human gait – jolly, purposeful, lively. And right now Stella's gait was certainly jolly. And purposeful. Lively, even.

"Honey!" Ron said. "You were a zombie!"

"Dad, have you inhaled the fumes from downstairs? The antidote is in the fucking air! All the zombies are turning! Even me!" She started dancing a Joan Jett jig, Ron Junior dancing along in her arms.

"AAAAAAAAAIR!" Ron Junior said, ecstatic to see his Mom and Dad.

"Wow," Ron said, as he lay back down on the bed.

"Are you okay, Dad?"

"Yeah, just a little rest. I've been dead for some time, apparently. I have no strength."

"I knew it!" Portly Elvis said. "I knew you were bluffing! I knew he was -" Maria pointed her pistol at PE. "Bluffing," he finished, sheepishly.

Maria finished tying Portly Elvis to the chair.

"Shall I kill him? I've never killed anybody before, but I almost killed myself," Maria said.

"Thank you, but no," Ron said. "Whatever happens to us, I want him to live a long life alone with his cowardice. And his portliness. Dude, mix in a salad once in awhile."

Ron heard his name being called from outside the broken window of the hotel room.

"Ron! Stella! Maria!"

He went over to see who was calling him and there, on the curb of the Vegas Strip below, was Jim, who was not dead after all. Jim, who was surrounded by four 1968 glossy white El Caminos with Cragar Rims.

"Oh, there you are," Jim said. "I saw the hotel's garage and there they were, four glossy white El Caminos. And I thought, there are four of us, if we ever find each other. Hello, each other!"

They all waved to Jim and he waved back.

"So I stole them, in case we ever bumped into each other. I guess we just did."

"Jim, you did something right," Stella said, a tear in her eye.

"Don't worry, I won't let it go to my head," Jim said.

Maria, with Ron Junior strapped into her Baby Bjorn, leaped from the window into Jim's arms. It's a good thing it was a garden level hotel room.

"You know, it's very strange," Ron said. "I have wanted to be a human for so long, now that it's over, I don't know what to do with the rest of my life."

Stella looked up at her dad, a loving smile on her face, and gave him the best idea ever. "Have you ever considered politics? You'd make a wonderful president, dad."

"Run for office? That's for crazy people," Ron said, but at that moment a seed was planted, deep down in his zombie soul, a seed that would lead to the greatest adventure of his life...

Stella jumped out the garden level window. It was more of a slight drop down, really, than a jump. Then Ron cleared his head and did the same.

Stella and Jim each took a glossy white El Camino and Ron, Maria, and Ron Junior shared one, leaving one behind. As they drove to freedom, dusk settled over the Vegas Valley and Ron and Maria knew they were finally safe. They leaned in to kiss. And as they reached for each other -

FIN?

AUTHOR'S ACKNOWLEDGMENTS

I would first and foremost like to again thank my writing group, without whose deadlines none of this would have happened. Your guidance and enthusiasm and willingness to slog through this ridiculous story while it was still a nascent zombie were invaluable. BRAINS.

A very special thanks again to Anthony (Vegas Ponch to my Vegas Jon) and the good bartenders and band members of Las Vegas, all of whom are in the book, one way or another. You all have made Vegas my second home and have become sacred friends. BRAINS.

A warm appreciation to my way-over-my-pay-grade development editor Jonna Gvejre, who somehow thought doing this was a good idea. BRAINS.

And a heartfelt admiration to cover designer extraordinaire Stewart Williams (www.stewartwilliamsdesign.com), who gives American Badass aesthetics that I could never dream of. You're fucking brilliant. BRAINS.

I also want to thank my family for putting up with my schedule: Vegas trips, writing sessions, Vegas trips, revision sessions, Vegas trips…I know not every husband/father get this kind of leeway, and I appreciate it very much. BRAINS.

Most importantly, thank you to everybody who read American Badass and left a comment or sent a message. It's amazing to know that A) people still read books and B) people still respond, at a visceral level, to humor in somewhat dark places. I believe we humans appreciate light at a whole other level when it's up against darkness, and I appreciate everybody who took the time to go on that journey with me the first time. You're also fucking brilliant. BRAINS!

Last but definitely not least, BRAINS to the people at Wooden Stake Press for taking a chance on me, *American Badass 2*, and Ron Watson. Again. This is another dream come true...

BRAAAAAIIIIIIIIIIIINNNNNNNNNNNSSSSSSSSS.

www.ronzombieamericanbadass.com

ABOUT THE AUTHOR

JEFF CHACON is the author of *American Badass,* a Vegas Zom-Com (a genre Jeff made up) novel (and soon to be film!), and co-author of the cult comedy classic *E-Male: of mouse and men.* He has appeared on theater and rock and roll stages all over Colorado and California in several productions and bands you've never heard of. He lives with his wife and kids in Denver…and visits Las Vegas. A lot.

www.theejeffchacon.com

ABOUT THE PRESS

Wooden Stake Press LLC publishes zombie books (obviously), humor, fantasy, magical realism, and more. Visit us on the web at www.woodenstakepress.com.

www.ingramcontent.com/pod-product-compliance
Lightning Source LLC
Chambersburg PA
CBHW020116180626
46812CB00006B/2619